Maurice Procter and The Murder Room

⟩⟩⟩ This title is part of The Murder Room, our series dedicated to making available out-of-print or hard-to-find titles by classic crime writers.

Crime fiction has always held up a mirror to society. The Victorians were fascinated by sensational murder and the emerging science of detection; now we are obsessed with the forensic detail of violent death. And no other genre has so captivated and enthralled readers.

Vast troves of classic crime writing have for a long time been unavailable to all but the most dedicated frequenters of second-hand bookshops. The advent of digital publishing means that we are now able to bring you the backlists of a huge range of titles by classic and contemporary crime writers, some of which have been out of print for decades.

From the genteel amateur private eyes of the Golden Age and the femmes fatales of pulp fiction, to the morally ambiguous hard-boiled detectives of mid twentieth-century America and their descendants who walk our twenty-first century streets, The Murder Room has it all. **⟩⟩⟩**

The Murder Room
Where Criminal Minds Meet

themurderroom.com

Maurice Procter 1906–1973

Born in Nelson, Lancashire, Maurice Procter attended the local grammar school and ran away to join the army at the age of fifteen. In 1927 he joined the police in Yorkshire and served in the force for nineteen years before his writing was published and he was able to write full-time. He was credited with an ability to write exciting stories while using his experience to create authentic detail. His procedural novels are set in Granchester, a fictional 1950s Manchester, and he is best known for his series characters, Detective Superintendent Philip Hunter and DCI Harry Martineau. Throughout his career, Procter's novels increased in popularity in both the UK and the US, and in 1960 *Hell is a City* was made into a film starring Stanley Baker and Billie Whitelaw. Procter was married to Winifred, and they had one child, Noel.

Philip Hunter

The Chief Inspector's Statement (1951)
   aka *The Pennycross Murders*
I Will Speak Daggers (1956)
   aka *The Ripper*

Chief Inspector Martineau

Hell is a City (1954)
   aka *Somewhere in This City*
The Midnight Plumber (1957)
Man in Ambush (1958)
Killer at Large (1959)

Devil's Due (1960)
The Devil Was Handsome (1961)
A Body to Spare (1962)
Moonlight Flitting (1963)
    aka *The Graveyard Rolls*
Two Men in Twenty (1964)
Homicide Blonde (1965)
    aka *Death has a Shadow*
His Weight in Gold (1966)
Rogue Running (1966)
Exercise Hoodwink (1967)
Hideaway (1968)

Standalone Novels
Each Man's Destiny (1947)
No Proud Chivalry (1947)
The End of the Street (1949)
Hurry the Darkness (1952)
Rich is the Treasure (1952)
    aka *Diamond Wizard*
The Pub Crawler (1956)
Three at the Angel (1958)
The Spearhead Death (1960)
Devil in Moonlight (1962)
The Dog Man (1969)

The Midnight Plumber

Maurice Procter

An Orion book

Copyright © Maurice Procter 1957

The right of Maurice Procter to be identified as the author of this work
has been asserted in accordance with the Copyright, Designs and Patents
Act 1988.

This edition published by
The Orion Publishing Group Ltd
Orion House
5 Upper St Martin's Lane
London WC2H 9EA

An Hachette UK company
A CIP catalogue record for this book is available from the British Library

ISBN 978 1 4719 0265 9

www.orionbooks.co.uk

CHAPTER ONE

THOUGH the place was within fifty yards of Granchester's brightest and busiest shopping street, it was not easy to find. But once the stranger had ventured along the dingy alley, he could walk past the little shop with its discreet sign, 'Your depot for Durex', and see a doorway where a dim lamp shone its light down on wet cobbles. Then if his eyes were tolerably good he would be able to read the sign beneath the lamp, and it would inform him that he had arrived at an establishment with the peculiar name of Jimmy Ganders. Inside (if he were fool enough to enter) he would find that there was nothing to support such whimsy. It was a gin palace, and less inviting than most: one long shabby room with a long bar, a row of iron-legged tables on the other side, running parallel with the bar, a dais at the far end, upon which an upright piano and a set of drums stood forlorn, doors in the corners on each side of the dais, marked respectively 'Ladies' and 'Gents', girlie advertisements for champagne cider on the walls, and little else save glasses, bottles, beer pumps, barmen and customers.

In Jimmy Ganders, at eight-thirty on a dark, drizzling September evening, there were some two dozen customers. Most of them were regulars. Others were there because the place had a certain notoriety: they were curious, or they had heard that willing girls could be found there. There was a group of pimply youths, talking in low voices, giggling, eyes all over the place. There were two American soldiers, talking earnestly to each other. There were lonely men, standing at the bar, taking covert glances at other men's women. Nearly all the women there seemed to be with their own men, but the circumstance did not stop them from casting bold glances around. They were not smart or beautiful women, but they were not without their attractions.

A young man entered, and as he walked to the bar he

1

surveyed the room with casual thoroughness. He nodded to one or two people, and his nods were returned without enthusiasm. He was an habitué of the place, and typical of its rougher sort. He was sturdy, fresh-faced, blond, blue-eyed. Physically he should have been attractive, but his eyes were cold and shallow, and the abnormal forward thrust of the lower jaw made his loose lips pout aggressively even in repose. He wore a baggy, dirty suit, a soiled, crumpled collar and a wrinkled tie, and an old van driver's cap. He ordered a pint of bitter and stood alone, drinking it.

The young man was followed into the room by an older man; a little, narrow-shouldered rat of a man in a shiny old blue serge suit, a grimy muffler, and a check cap worn at a jaunty angle. The red-rimmed eyes in his sly, pinched face were busy from the moment he entered, but his glance roved no more after it had rested upon the young man he followed. He stopped at the bar a yard or two away from his quarry, without appearing to have noticed him. He shivered in his threadbare suit, and announced to the barman who came that he would treat himself to rum and peppermint.

He received his drink, sipped it, grimaced with pleasure, and looked at his neighbour. "Hallo, Ewart lad," he said in glad surprise, moving nearer.

The young fellow looked down at him with tolerant unwelcome. "How do," he grunted.

"Nasty night," the little man said, and Ewart nodded.

There was a brief silence. The little man looked around the room and remarked: "Quiet in here."

"Quiet everywhere," Ewart replied, and he permitted himself a small, secret grin.

"You're telling me," was the rejoinder. "Everybody's scared stiff."

"I'm not scared."

"Well, I'm not, come to that. My nose is clean."

"Is it? You're Martineau's grasshopper. Everybody knows that."

The little man was injured. "Nay, Ewart! I never sung to a cop in me life. I did me stretch at Farways, didn't I? Does that sound as if I'd grass?"

Ewart did not reply. The little man, whose name was Willis Cooper, contemplated his drink before he took another sip. Then he asked: "How's the job going?"

"Not so bad," Ewart replied. He was—officially—out of work, and he knew that the other man knew it.

"They tell me they're short of labourers in the plumbing trade?" Willis ventured, watching closely.

Ewart did not react, except to say without interest: "I never done no plumbing." But he could see Willis in the back-bar mirror. Through the mirror he had seen Willis enter the room, and he had grimly watched the make-believe of an accidental meeting. Willis, who was subtle, never thought of the mirror. Mirrors are so obvious.

Willis was slightly disappointed, and he began to wonder if he had got hold of a cock-and-bull tale. But his insatiable curiosity drove him. He tried another seemingly innocent question.

"Have you and Tom Egan fallen out, or what?" he wanted to know. "When I saw you both in the Prodigal Son you didn't seem to be speaking."

"I've no quarrel with Tom, but we never were right friendly."

"Not friendly enough to talk in a bar, but friendly enough to be gabbing very confidential in a back-alley off Bishopsgate," said Willis in quick triumph.

Ewart hooded his light eyes. "So what?" he demanded calmly. "What about it?"

"Nowt, lad, nowt," Willis disclaimed. He sipped his drink thoughtfully.

Then it was Ewart who spoke. "Are you all right for cash?" he asked softly.

"Why, you got some to spare?"

"No, I could do with some."

"Sorry, I've got none to lend. I'll give you a winner for tomorrow, though. Hammerfest. I've followed it through the season."

"Hammerfest. What's it at?"

"Eights. And it'll win," said Willis with certainty. But he seemed to have become bored with Ewart. His manner had changed. He finished his drink, said "Cheerio" without friendliness, and went out.

In the mirror Ewart watched the departure. Then he stood in thought. "The plumbing trade," he muttered. He drank off his beer in one long swig, flung a curt word to the barman, and followed Willis.

When he looked outside, the alley was deserted. He ran a-tiptoe to the end, and peered cautiously round the corner into Lacy Street. He saw Willis's small figure moving along under the bright lights. His tense attitude relaxed a little. Willis was not going towards Police Headquarters, at any rate. But he could be going to keep a street-corner appointment with a detective. Or he could use a telephone. Ewart crossed the road, and continued to follow at a safe distance.

He saw Willis walk past a public telephone kiosk, and he sighed for another danger averted. Now, unless there was to be a meeting with a policeman, there was no great hurry. Willis Cooper's insatiable curiosity had not yet led him to discover enough to excite his equally strong impulse to tell what he knew.

Willis turned the corner from Lacy Street into Tyburn Street, and Ewart guessed where he was going. When Willis went along a narrow street called Higgitt's Passage, the other man waited a full minute before he followed. In Higgitt's Passage there was a small inn which went by the name of The Prodigal Son. It stood at the junction of the passage and a narrow back street which ran parallel to the main street. Here were the walls of the backyards of shops. Ewart climbed the wall of the nearest yard and stood upon it, so that he could look across the passage downward into the lighted bar of the inn.

He stood quite still upon the wall, his excellent eyes glinting with some strong excitement. He could see half a dozen of the customers in the inn. He saw Willis in conversation with a man of powerful physique, clad in flannel trousers and a gaudy yellow and black sweater. Willis was talking; the big man was saying little in reply. As he watched, Ewart curled his thin lips and spat out a profane word.

He jumped down from the wall and hurried into Lacy

Street, to the nearest telephone box. He entered the box and dialled a number he knew.

"Hallo," someone answered. "Who is speaking?"

"I'm needing a plumber," Ewart replied, knowing that his voice would be recognized. "Have you a man available?"

"I may have," said the person at the other end. "What's your trouble?"

Ewart turned in the box so that he could look across Lacy Street. "I'm having trouble with a W.C.," he said.

"A water closet?" the voice said patiently, but as yet without understanding. "What's the matter with it?"

"It leaks. I'm afraid it'll do some damage."

"Is it a serious leak?"

"Well, *I* think it's serious."

"What does it require?"

"It wants taking out altogether. You'll never repair it."

"Have we been called to this water closet before?"

"I prefer to call it a W.C. You know it all right. You looked at it last year," said Ewart. And at that moment he saw Willis Cooper come from Tyburn Street and walk up Lacy Street.

"I think I know the one," said the Plumber. "Let's see, what's the address?"

"You know, just up Lacy Street. I'm looking at the blasted thing now. I'd like you to attend to this matter as soon as you possibly can, otherwise there might be trouble with the sanitary authorities."

"I'll send a man straight away," said the Plumber.

Ewart left the phone box and went to the Prodigal Son. He entered the bar like a warm breeze. "Evening all," he said cheerily, and then he looked at the clock. "Five past nine?" he queried in a shocked voice. "I'd no idea it was so far on. Here, Doug, is your clock right?"

Douglas Savage, who managed the inn for his aged mother, looked up sharply from the glass of beer which he was drawing.

"The clock's all right," he rasped. "What's the gag? Are you drawing my attention to the time?"

Ewart was hurt. "Cor!" he said. "I don't know what's

5

come over everybody. You can't ask a civil question without somebody biting your head off."

Doug eyed him, and remained silent.

"Oh, forget the perishing time, will you?" Ewart jeered, aware that everyone in the room could hear him.

"I'll forget it, all right," said Doug grimly. "You don't drag me into nothing."

Ewart said: "Fill me a pint and stop nattering." He moved along the little bar to the big man in the sweater. The big man acknowledged his approach with the faintest of nods.

"Have a pint, Tom," said Ewart.

"No thanks," said the big man coldly. "I'm just going."

"Oh, stay and have a pint, Tom," Ewart insisted.

Tom gave him a quick stare. "All right," he assented with bad grace. "I'll just stay for the odd one."

Ewart ordered the drink, and looked around the room. He smiled and spoke to a girl he knew. Then he spoke to a small, dark, dangerous-looking youth who sat at a table with a young blonde of remarkable shapeliness. "Hallo, Alex," he said, but the little desperado only scowled at him.

"What's the matter with you?" demanded Tom Egan in a low voice. "You drunk, or something?"

"Never more sober," was the almost inaudible reply.

"You know we're not supposed to be seen together."

"We are tonight. What was Willis Cooper talking about?"

"Oh, this and that. He asked if I'd seen you lately."

"He didn't say he'd just seen me?"

"No."

"He's sniffing, Tom."

"Sure, he always is. He'll spill all he knows, but he don't know anything."

"He's very fly. I think he's got hold of something. He's getting warm."

"Well, he can always be cooled, can't he?"

"He sure can. That's why you and I are staying right here in this bar till closing time. Alex stays too. Give him the wire if he looks like going."

"I get you," said Tom. "Good health." He raised his mug

of beer and drank deeply. Then he belched lengthily, and said: "You want to be careful, Ewart. That 'Is the clock right?' stunt of yours was too much of a good thing. It'll make people wonder. The boss won't like it."

"Why, will you tell him?"

"No," said Tom. "But somebody might."

Ewart thought that the business of establishing an alibi had been very neatly done. "Ah, you're crackers!" he said with contempt. He was very cunning, but not very intelligent.

CHAPTER TWO

DETECTIVE SERGEANT DEVERY opened the door of Chief Inspector Martineau's office and looked in.

"Fatal accident in Union Street," he said. "Ten minutes ago."

."Why tell me?" Martineau retorted. "That's a Traffic job."

"I thought you might be interested, sir. The driver left the car and ran away. The dead man is Willis Cooper."

Martineau put down his pen. "Get a car," he said.

In Union Street, Devery parked the plain C.I.D. car behind an ambulance, and the two detective officers pushed through a crowd of people who had gathered around the brightly-lit windows of a department store. The big shop was at the junction of Union Street and Lacy Street.

Across the broad sidewalk, with its radiator jammed against a thick marble pillar of the building, was an old black car. One front door of the car, on the driver's side, was hanging wide open. Three uniformed policemen were keeping the crowd away from the car. Two ambulance men and a nurse waited near.

One of the policemen, a sergeant, touched his helmet when he saw Martineau. "Nothing has been moved or handled, sir," he said. "The man is as dead as a dodo, so I left him where he was till you'd seen him."

7

Martineau went to look, and Devery peered over his shoulder. Jammed between steel and stone were the remains of Willis Cooper. There was no doubt he could not possibly have been alive. His head had been crushed between the front bumper of the car and the unyielding masonry. His expression of snarling desperate terror was fixed, like the grin on the face of a slain rat. Willis had died appropriately.

"It's murder all right," said Martineau. "Number Three. Three right good informers. We won't get a whisper out of anybody after this. The town will be as silent as a grave-yard."

"How did they catch him that way, down on the ground?" Devery wanted to know.

"That's what makes me so sure that it was deliberate murder. See the unnatural mobility when I move his feet. They hit him while he was standing or walking here, and broke both his legs. They backed off and he sank down on one elbow. Then they hit him again, and crushed his head. Look closely, the body is still held there, leaning on one elbow."

Devery looked. "They're *bloody* cruel," he said. "Poor old Willis. He was a useful little scoundrel."

Martineau nodded, without much sympathy. He had to make use of informers, but he had no kind feeling for them. However, his feelings were even less kind for the men who murdered them. Now there were three murders to clear; three separate crimes which probably were, in a sense, one and the same crime. The culprits were the same, responsible for three murders in a few weeks just as they were responsible for a dozen major robberies during the same period. Some tightly organized gang was enriching itself at the expense of the city, and at the same time making itself safe by silencing the sources of police information. The underworld of Granchester, city of a million people in the centre of a close urban population of several millions, was terrified. Thieves, prostitutes and tough rowdies alike were afraid to talk about crime of any sort. Those who were vocationally on the fringe of the underworld—bookmakers and their clerks, runners and tictac men, publicans, barmaids, layabouts, bouncers, newsboys, hawkers—were behaving with extreme caution. The town had buttoned its lip.

Two more policemen arrived, and Martineau said to the sergeant: "Push this crowd back, right back. And keep the road clear."

The sergeant and his men did as they were told, and soon the spectators were watching from a decent distance. The sergeant returned, and Martineau asked: "Who was first on the job?"

"Me," said the sergeant. "I was coming down Lacy Street. I heard the crash, but there was no sound of broken glass and I didn't run. I just walked fast, like. When I got here I asked for witnesses, but nobody would admit having seen the actual incident."

"I'm not surprised. Even the general public is getting the wind up now. Nobody wants to be involved. What about the driver?"

"Somebody must have seen him. There are always people about here at this time of night. But nobody would say they'd seen him."

"Too bad," said Martineau. "Go around asking again, will you? Somebody might change his mind."

The sergeant went away, and C.I.D. men with cameras arrived. Photographs were taken, and the car was moved. More photographs were taken, and then the ambulance men took charge of the body. Devery went with them, to see what Willis Cooper had had in his pockets. Martineau arranged for the car to be towed to Headquarters, and he went there himself.

At Headquarters, with the murder car under cover and under guard until daylight, Martineau learned that the car had not been in the possession of the murderer for more than a few minutes. It had been stolen a short distance away, a little while before the crime. Probably no finger-print other than the owner's would be found upon it. The owner would be questioned, and he would be found to have no connexion with the crime. It was going to be a murder without clues, like the two which had preceeded it.

The only information Martineau had was something

which Willis Cooper had gabbled over the telephone that very morning. He had said: "There's summat about a plumber. There's a plumber mixed up in it somewhere, but I don't know how." That was all. And now Martineau had a list of all the master plumbers in Granchester on his desk. There were hundreds of them, and each master plumber had two, three, four, or up to a dozen men. To go nosing around among a lot of plumbers was not the inspector's intention, but the list would remain there, on the desk, until the case was cleared.

Perhaps, this evening, Cooper had learned something else, and had been silenced before he could transmit his knowledge to the police. That was a pity. Martineau sat in his study and meditated about informers. They were fairly harmless little men as a rule, petty criminals usually. Strange people, they seemed to value the contemptuous friendship of police officers. They accepted money for their information, and they expected as much protection from other police officers as one policeman could give, but money and protection were not their main objects. In helping the police they sought to gratify some inner urge which had nothing to do with righteousness. There was vanity: they were proud of their own cleverness in getting information. And there was also a queer desire to have a part, though a secret one, in actual police work. They were usually small men. Martineau had heard more than one of them say: "I'd a-been a copper if I'd been big enough."

The big policeman grinned ruefully. One thing was very clear. Police informers were a dying race in Granchester.

His thoughts turned to the other side, the men who were doing the killing. There seemed to be a highly organized gang, and—apart from the race-track gangs—that was a most uncommon thing in England. There was a guiding brain obviously, and a hand strong enough to impose discipline upon men, who of all men, were the least amenable to discipline. The discipline was there, all right. The gang was doing extremely well financially, but no matter how closely the police watched they saw no flash money, no heavy spending. The man who could prevent *all* the members of a mob of thieves with money in their pockets from following their natural inclinations—drink, women and horses—was a born disciplinarian.

"He must have put the fear of God into 'em," the inspector mused.

Since there was no line of inquiry upon which to work, the Granchester police were doing what they could in the way of observation and prevention. The man on the beat had come into his own. It was not even hoped that the man on the beat would succeed in catching the criminals while they were actually committing a crime, but it was expected that he would eventually see or hear enough to give his superiors a lead.

The Chief Constable, shocked and worried by the run of serious crime in his district, organized his manpower with a ruthless efficiency which had little regard for comfort. In the daytime, traffic points were controlled by police-women, or left vacant. A few men in uniform patrolled the main streets, showing themselves as much as possible so that there would be no suspicion in the public mind that there were not many officers about. In the evenings, unpaid Special Constables were able to help. They patrolled in pairs, with instructions to keep out of trouble and inform Head-quarters of the least suspicious occurrence. Area patrol cars prowled about the suburbs, and a van with a reserve squad of men waited for calls at Headquarters.

Then at nine o'clock each night the main body of the force went into action. For beat working the group system was adopted. Four squads of men, each squad supplied with a car and commanded by a sergeant, 'worked' the city area by area, moving apparently at random from one district to another when they had examined every accessible lock and window latch. Wherever they happened to be, they gave an impression of great police activity. Wherever they happened to be, no criminal could operate. They were noticed, and they were meant to be noticed.

The remainder of the force, nearly a thousand keen, well-trained men, each one eager to stop the nuisance, clear the crimes, and get some rest, turned out in plain clothes and faded into the night. Darkly clad, rubber shod, hugging the shadows, they moved silently and carefully, watching and listening. They showed no lights; they tried no doors unless for a reason. They just lurked, looked and listened.

It was not possible to pick out property to be particularly guarded. The men whom Martineau was beginning to call the Plumber's men sought only money and jewellery. The jeweller's shops could easily be covered, but in the city centre there was money everywhere. There were thousands of shops, stores and offices, with thousands of safes containing money. And money and jewellery were to be found elsewhere than in the centre of the city. The suburbs were wide. It was in the shrubberies and under the garden trees of rich houses that many of the plain-clothes men lurked.

The members of the C.I.D., already in plain clothes, did their share of night prowling. Even Martineau kept the dreary vigil for several nights. As a chief inspector he had a free run of the entire police district, going where he liked without instruction. It was he who first made contact with the Plumber.

At half-past two in the morning, two days after the murder of Willis Cooper, Martineau stood in the grounds of Elms House, the home of Sir Clement Wesley, city alderman and cotton millionaire. There was a little breeze rustling in the trees. There had been rain, but now the clouds were thinning, and wan moonlight filtered through them to relieve the darkness. Martineau was wet, and his feet were sodden, and he wished it was morning. He stood well back among trees at the side of the house, so that he had some chance of observing an approach from either front or rear.

He was trying to convince himself that there would be no harm in lighting a cigarette when he became aware of movement under the trees skirting the drive, and he saw that someone was walking on the grass there and keeping in the shadows.

He waited, without excitement. The newcomer was moving in his direction, avoiding the open space in front of the house and staying under the trees. Then he stopped, and Martineau began to stalk him. He thought that the man might be a fellow officer, but he did not intend to disclose his presence until he was sure. He proceeded slowly and carefully, keeping well behind the other man so that no movement of his could be seen. He was within four yards, directly in rear, when the man began to move away from him. Martineau saw him in silhouette against the faintly moonlit forecourt of the house. He knew that soldierly bearing. It was the Chief Constable himself, one of the most important police officials in the country, out doing the work of a P.C. in time of need. The inspector made a slight sibilant noise to attract attention.

The Chief turned, quite unstartled, and came to him. "Hallo, Martineau," he said in a matter-of-fact whisper. "You're out on the job, too?"

"Yes, sir."

"Have you been round this house?"

"Yes, sir. Several times."

"Have you been watching one house all the time?" the Chief wanted to know, with an edge of disapproval in his voice.

"Yes, sir."

"Why?"

"You know who lives here?"

"I certainly do. I've had many a good dinner in that house. Clem Wesley would snigger a bit if he knew I was out here in the middle of the night, staring up at his window."

There was a brief silence, and then the Chief said: "But why this one place? Lady Wesley was never a woman for wanting a lot of jewels, and Sir Clement once told me that he doesn't keep much money in the house."

"Perhaps he told you that, sir, but did he tell the Press?"

"Of course not. I see what you mean. He's a very rich man."

"That isn't it. There was a picture in the *Evening Guardian* the other day."

"I remember. Some Americans."

"Canadians, sir. A Canadian gentleman and his wife, friends of Sir Clement. It can be assumed that they're very rich. In the picture the lady was wearing a string of pearls worth a fortune if they were real. And it said that she owns the Witwater Diamond, which is supposed to be about as big as a duck egg."

"So?"

"These Canadians are Sir Clement's guests for a few days. It was there in the local paper for everyone to read."

"I congratulate you, Martineau. Not another man in the force saw the possibilities of that. You think our gang of thieving murderers might have a bash at getting the Witwater Diamond?"

"Not to mention other trinkets they could pick up, sir. I couldn't watch the house in the daytime to see if anyone was casing it. I'm too well-known for that. But I put a policewoman on to hang around in civvies. She has seen nothing out of the way."

"Well, that's something. You *may* be wasting your time, you know. Lady Wesley won't have a dog on the place, she has a terror of them. But she also has a terror of burglars. Sir Clement has the finest burglar alarm system I've ever seen. It doesn't run from the mains. It can't be got at from outside at all."

"Only from the inside?" was Martineau's polite query.

"That's right. I believe there's a switch somewhere near the front door."

Martineau made no comment about that, and the Chief went on: "Yours is a good idea, all the same. I'll set my office staff watching the newspapers for that sort of thing. It might put us one jump ahead. By the way, are you armed?"

Martineau was surprised. "Firearms haven't been issued, sir."

"I know that. But aren't you carrying a staff?"

"No sir."

The Chief fingered the short, heavy truncheon in his raincoat pocket. It was an issue staff which he had borrowed from stores. He remembered hearing that Martineau was a very formidable man. The hardest hitter in the force, it was reported. "You should carry a staff on a job of this sort," he said, but not very severely.

14

Martineau, who never carried a staff, discreetly made no reply. For a while nothing was said. The two men listened to the rustle of the trees, at night one of the loneliest sounds on earth. Then they heard a car.

"Somebody's out late," the Chief commented.

They stood listening as the car came along the road. It seemed to decrease speed as it approached the open gateway of Elms House. Not presuming to tell the Chief what to do, Martineau drew back into the shrubbery. His superior officer did likewise.

The car came up the drive at speed, and circled to a stop at the front door. Its lighted sign, 'Police', was clearly visible. Obviously the driver was not on any sort of patrol. He was in a hurry.

A man in motor patrol uniform leaped from the car and pounded on the door. Then he found a bell button and leaned on it. Then he pounded the door again. A light appeared in a front bedroom.

"Why didn't they phone from Headquarters?" Martineau murmured in the Chief's ear.

"Perhaps the phone didn't rouse anybody. Shall we go and see what is the matter?"

"Suppose the wires have been cut? I'd advise staying here for a while, sir. We shall be able to hear what it's all about."

Presently the porch light was switched on, and the door was opened by a tall man in a dressing-gown. He was not old but his hair shone like silver under the light.

"That's Deakin, the butler," the Chief whispered.

They heard the constable speaking. "This is Sir Clement Wesley's house?"

The butler made a reply, and the P.C. went on: "I think you'd better. Tell him that the Wood Street warehouse is on fire, and going like a furnace. If you like I'll wait for him and run him into town."

The butler spoke again. The policeman said: "You'll drive him into town? All right, I'll go back."

The constable returned to his car. "Down, sir!" Martineau hissed, grasping the Chief's arm. They crouched. The car's headlights swept over the bushes as it completed its circle and sped away. Then they were in darkness again. The bedroom light went out.

The butler closed the front door, leaving the porch light on. The Chief started to say something, but his arm was pressed again.

"We've got company," Martineau whispered, with his mouth to the Chief's ear. "Somebody moved, over on the other side, near that yew hedge. Whoever it is, he must have come the back way."

They waited, staying quite still. The light reappeared in the front bedroom. Evidently the butler had informed Sir Clement. A minute later the front door was opened again. The butler emerged. He had put on trousers and a dark overcoat, and he wore a bowler hat perfectly straight upon his head. He went around the house towards the garages, leaving the front door open. As soon as he had gone, four dark figures crept out of the shadow of the yew hedge and entered the house.

"They're wearing masks!" was the Chief's whispered exclamation.

"Do we tackle 'em now?" Martineau wanted to know.

The Chief pondered. "I think we have time to get them right," he said. "They'll hide somewhere until Sir Clement has gone, and then they'll go to work. We'll get some assistance out here and collar the lot of them. Where is there a public telephone around here?"

Martineau told him, and advised him that the thieves would have look-outs. "They'll have a car not far away," he said. "If we go back to the wall I can help you to get over into the grounds of Wyvern Lodge. Then if you go out of the back gate you'll see the phone box on the corner."

They made their way to the side wall of the garden. Martineau made a stirrup of his hands and the Chief got a leg over the wall and dropped down on the other side. The inspector returned to his post, reflecting that the thieves might have completed their task before the police reinforcements could gather. And there were at least four of them. He began to wish that he had put a staff in his pocket, as the Chief had done.

16

He made his way around the side of the house until he came to an archway which led to the backyard. He looked into the yard. Over at the far side the butler was getting a car out of the garage. Elsewhere all was quiet and still. He guessed that the butler would be under observation, so he did not dare to approach him. He crossed the yard to where he saw the roof of a greenhouse glimmering faintly. Somewhere around there, he hoped, he would find gardening tools. A spade or a mattock would be a good enough weapon.

He found a shed behind the greenhouse. The door was not locked. He opened it and slipped inside, and stood listening in pitch darkness. Then he took a torch from his pocket and risked a quick look around. He saw a dusty profusion of spades, hoes, pots, canes, balls of twine, sacks and boxes of fertilizer. A bench occupied one side of the shed, and on the bench there was the head of a woodsman's axe. Beside the axe-head there was a new helve, waiting to be fitted. Martineau picked up the thirty-inch length of tough wood and balanced it in his hand. It was a better weapon than a policeman's truncheon.

He went back, through the archway and along the side of the house. When he reached the front corner he stopped and listened. He crouched, and with his head not much above knee level he looked round the corner. He was in time to see Sir Clement Wesley get into the rear seat of a Bentley car. The butler, acting as chauffeur, closed the door of the car upon him and took the driving seat. Martineau shrank away from the corner as the car was driven away.

He saw the car's tail lights vanish through the distant gateway, and he saw trees in its headlight glare as it sped along the road. Then he looked up as a light sprang out from the windows of the big corner bedroom above him. Apparently a window was open, because he heard a man's voice quite clearly. The accent was North American. "Hey you! What the hell are you doing in here?"

He heard the reply: "Sit tight, chum, and you won't get hurt. All we want is a few bits-and-bats. Where do you keep the Witwater Diamond?"

"In Toronto, in a safe-deposit. You're out of luck."

17

"All right. If we can't find the diamond, we'll take what there is. Steady! This gun is loaded. If you try to put one foot out of bed I'll blow your head off. Go on, kid, see what you can find. I'll watch this fellow."

Gun or no gun, Martineau wished that he was up there with his axe handle. He was about to make his way to the front door when he heard another car. He remained in concealment as it came up the drive and stopped at the front door. As it stopped, the driver touched his horn button just once, by accident or design. Thereafter, he waited with his engine running, and his headlights glaring in the direction of Martineau's corner.

Martineau turned and ran lightly round the house, because he could only approach the car from the rear. As he ran he took out his penknife and held it open in his left hand. He thought that he might be able to slit the tyres of the car. He also thought that he would put the driver out of action if there was half a chance.

He was too late. When he came round to the front of the house again, all the front bedrooms were showing light, and there was a thin monotonous screaming which was probably Lady Wesley in hysterics. The raiders had been very quick. Light streamed from the front door, and men were emerging and running to the car.

Martineau ran forward, and now he had a police whistle in his left hand instead of his knife. He was hoping that a surprise attack might spread panic among men whose nerves were bound to be taut with strain. He thought that he might cause some confusion, knock over one or two men, and scare the others away. He was determined to take at least one prisoner.

At first he ran in silence. Then he was seen, and someone shouted: "Look out!" A split second later he was among them, hitting out with the helve. His whistle was between his teeth and he was blowing it like a maniac. Shouts and shots added to the din. The first man out of the house scrambled to safety in the car. Martineau swung at the second man. The man ducked, but a glancing blow sent him reeling. The third man blocked a blow with his forearm, and dropped a pistol he had been holding. The fourth man nipped smartly around behind Martineau and dived into the car.

Somewhere there was a ringing command: "Hold 'em, Martineau! Come on, men!"

Someone in the car had fired several shots at Martineau, but the big policeman had been moving about too quickly to make a good target. Now there was another shot, and he felt his right arm go numb. The bullet had struck the axe-helve and knocked it out of his hand.

Someone in the car was exhorting the thieves to get in. The man who had been clipped on the head made it with a short, wobbly run, and was dragged inside. Number Three, the man with the damaged arm, was still trying to get around Martineau. There was another shot, which did not seem to hit anybody. In the middle distance the Chief was still shouting as he charged forward.

Martineau stretched his long left arm and gathered Number Three to him as if he loved him. The man cursed painfully, and struck out. He was caught off balance and turned around, and the arm went about his neck in a choking grip. He was held like a shield in front of his captor.

There was a sharp command: "Get moving!" and the car shot away around the circular head of the drive. The Chief, coming up at a run, had to leap sideways to avoid being knocked down.

The car's headlights were too revealing. And the man who commanded the raid had not panicked altogether. Apparently he observed that the Chief was not supported by a body of men. Instead of going away down the drive, the car made a full circle and returned to the front door. Martineau saw the move and started to drag his prisoner back into the house. The car stopped at the door. There was a single shot. The prisoner slumped, and was only held up by Martineau's strength. The car sped away, and this time it did not return.

The Chief came up. "Are you hit?" he asked breathlessly.

"No," said Martineau. "Is that car going to get away?"

"I hope not. It's inside a cordon. Men and cars are closing in from all directions."

Martineau lowered his prisoner gently, until he was sitting propped in a corner of the doorway. He pulled down the mask, and the porch light shone down upon the man's slack face.

"He's dead!" the Chief exclaimed.

Martineau nodded. "I felt the bullet hit him. I guessed he'd had it."

"Well, if they shoot at you and kill one of their own men, it's murder just the same. Do you know this man?"

"Yes. His name was Ewart Thompson. He was a bad boy. He had quite a record."

A big man in dressing-gown and slippers emerged from the house. He slipped quietly past the group in the doorway and picked up the axe-helve. He seemed ready to use it.

"Steady," said Martineau rather wearily. "Police."

The man relaxed. He looked down at the dead man and saw the silk scarf which had been used as a mask. "I see you've got one of them," he said with satisfaction. Martineau recognized his accent. He was Sir Clement's guest.

"I've been trying to call the police with that nine-nine-nine business," the Canadian said. "The line was dead. Do you figure they cut the wires?"

"I expect so," the Chief replied. "What did they take from you?"

"All my wife's stuff. But I'm not grumbling: it's all insured. They didn't bother to take my watch, and they didn't stay to look for cash."

"No, they were very quick. Unfortunately. Otherwise we'd have collared the lot of 'em."

"I'm surprised," the Canadian said. "I thought this sort of thing didn't happen in England."

"Gunplay, you mean? Oh, it does happen, but not often. When we've caught this lot, and hanged them, there'll be peace for a while."

A police car came up the drive at speed. The Chief went towards it as it stopped.

The Canadian eyed Martineau curiously. He nodded in

20

the direction of the corpse. "Did *you* give it to him?" he asked.

Martineau shook his head. "I was holding him. One of his own mates shot him."

"Intentionally, do you mean? To stop him talking? Gee, that's rough."

Martineau looked towards the city. There was a dull red glow in the sky.

"Very rough," he agreed. "I think this mob must be something quite out of the ordinary." He pointed. "That's how rough this crowd is. They set fire to a million-pound warehouse in order to steal a few diamonds."

CHAPTER THREE

THE value of the jewels stolen from the Canadian woman amounted to more than thirty thousand dollars, which, as her husband remarked, was ten thousand pounds and then some.

A crime yielding so much plunder to the thieves, and a murder to boot, is enough to make the C.I.D. chief of any police force in the world feel slightly sick. Detective Chief Superintendent Clay looked at the report and moaned. "You should've stopped 'em before they got their hands on the stuff," he said to Martineau. "You should've broke 'em up."

"The Chief Constable said 'No'," Martineau replied blandly.

Clay looked round to see if his office door was closed, then he said: "I don't know why the Chief wants to interfere so much. Why doesn't he go to bed at nights like any other Chief, instead of snooping around like a cabby at a christening?"

Martineau was silent. He did not think that it was quite fair to criticize a man who was doing his best. Probably Clay too, realized that he was being somewhat unjust, because he changed the subject and spoke in a more cheerful tone.

"There's one thing about it," he said. "The killing of Ewart Thompson will shake 'em. It never does a team any good to shoot through their own goal. No matter what the boss mobster says, they'll wonder if Thompson was intentionally rubbed out because the police had him. They'll be thinking it might happen to any one of 'em. That's very bad for morale."

"Oh, they'll let the Plumber talk them round," said Martineau. "If the gang is made up of mugs like Thompson, he'll have no trouble. First he'll say how sorry he is, because he shot the wrong man. Then he'll say that Thompson wasn't much good anyway. Then he'll point out that Thompson's share makes an extra bonus for everybody. Phrased diplomatically, it'll make a good enough tale for a crowd of loaf-heads. They'll believe what they want to believe."

"Not in a case like that, they won't. That sort of thing is bound to leave them uneasy."

"Well, it probably won't happen again, and as time goes by they'll forget it."

Clay glared. "As time goes by? Dammit all, man! I want those blasted scoundrels in the cells before any more time goes by."

"Naturally," was Martineau's cool reply.

Clay snorted, and looked at the report again. Property recovered was set down at fifteen hundred pounds. That was the total value of Lady Wesley's jewels, which had been found in Ewart Thompson's pocket. Fifteen hundred pounds seemed to be a small sum when it was compared with ten thousand.

"You grabbed the wrong man," he grumbled.

"Yes. Just my bad luck."

"You did very well to be there at all," came the gruff admission. "Instead of running around aimlessly you used a bit of common sense. Did you find anything else on the body?"

"A reasonable amount of money, none of it traceable. One Colt automatic pistol, the property of Uncle Sam. American security at Burtonwood is working on it. Very likely it was flogged to Thompson by some G.I. There was nothing else of any interest."

"What about his family?"

"No mother. The father has married again and lives at Boyton. He hadn't seen Ewart for years, and hadn't wanted to. There are three married sisters, all quite respectable. The three brothers-in-law had no use for Ewart at all."

"His record?"

"Bad, almost from the start. Approved schools, Borstal, and H.M. Prison, in that order. But until recently he was only a small-timer. His longest stretch was eighteen months for shopbreaking. That was his last sentence. He came out of Farways Prison last March."

"Who were his pals?"

"Now you're asking me something. He must have had friends of a sort, but they aren't admitting it. Nobody will admit having seen him anywhere, at any time. Nobody is talking. The whole town is gagged."

"You've tried to trace his movements, I suppose."

"Sure. I can't get to know a thing."

Clay had to leave it at that. "Keep at it," was all he could say, and his subordinate left him.

Back in his own office Martineau reflected that the fire at the Wood Street warehouse had caused damage to the extent of fifty thousand pounds, but it seemed to worry Clay a good deal less than the robbery. Nevertheless, it was an obvious case of arson. A two-gallon can of petrol, with the cap removed, had been thrown through a ground floor window of the warehouse, and a blazing rag had been thrown after it.

Martineau considered the simple planning of the Wesley job. The Plumber had known, or had suspected, that Elms House had an invulnerable burglar alarm. But a quiet and speedy entry had been necessary, so that the Canadian guest would not have time to arm himself or barricade the door of the bedroom occupied by himself and his wife. Therefore someone within the house had to be induced to switch off the alarm and open the door. So the telephone wires had been cut and a fire started at one of Sir Clement's warehouses. The police had informed Sir Clement. The butler had left the door open while he went for a car, and the thieves had crept into the house. If things had not happened in exactly that way, they could have forced their way in at pistol point as Sir Clement was emerging. They had done the job and got away; or at least most of them had. And then what? They had got out of a police cordon undetected. The get-away car had not been seen after leaving Elms House, until it was found abandoned a few hours later. Therefore it seemed likely that the Plumber's escape route had been carefully worked out in advance. He had found some unconsidered lane or back street which was not likely to be blocked by policemen keeping a cordon. He had not raced home: he had sneaked home.

Martineau tried to recall every impression of the hectic half-minute at Sir Clement's front door. He could remember men uniformly clad in dark clothes, with dark scarves or kerchiefs masking their faces. One of them had been a big fellow, he thought. The man who had escaped after a tap on the head had been of medium height and medium build. The fellow who had dodged him by going behind him had been short and thickset, he believed, but he could not be quite sure. He had heard a voice, but it had been full of strain and urgency. It was doubtful if it would be recognizable in ordinary circumstances. That was all. It was little upon which to continue an investigation.

Four murders now. One thief and three stool pigeons—George Allott, Tommy Straw, and Willis Cooper. All four men had moved more or less in the same orbit. They had all been poor uneducated men with unsettled and immoral lives; irresponsible men who had yet envied those who had the rewards of responsibility. They had all used the same haunts, whether pubs, billiard halls, cheap restaurants or snack bars. To look for one of them in any one place was to look for them all.

Still, Martineau and Devery, assigned to those four murders, worked separately to cover more ground. It was a long time since Martineau had done his own leg work, but Clay would not let him have the men to do it for him.

The wily superintendent knew quite well what he was about. Martineau was a born detective. At times of emergency he was better employed in actual inquiry rather than in supervising the work of others.

Devery, too, was a first-class investigator, and he was also a 'lucky' one. He had a talent for creating trouble of the right sort for a policeman, or of being on the spot when trouble started. It was Devery who sniffed the first faint scent of the trail which was to lead to the Plumber.

At noontime on the day following the night of the Wesley job, Devery saw Richard Costello getting out of his car in front of the Northland Hotel. His glance took in everything about the man. Dixie Costello was worth a policeman's attention at any time.

But Dixie could not openly be called a criminal. He had no record at Police Headquarters, not even for motoring offences. And yet he was known as a boss mobster and a racketeer by Granchester people, by people in the underworld of London and other big cities, and by bookmakers who set up their stands on race courses up and down the country. He was a race-gang leader, but he no longer settled disputes about betting pitches by leading his mob in action. When territorial trouble arose at the races, Dixie travelled with a suitable escort to London or Birmingham, or wherever it was necessary to go, and settled the matter with sweet reason and a passing mention of the force at his disposal. Men with razors, bludgeons and, if necessary, firearms were available, but Dixie preferred to get his own way through forceful diplomacy.

During the years of austerity Dixie had been a power in the black market, and much of his profit, ostensibly acquired by successful betting, had been invested in legitimate business. He had been heard to say that he did not mind paying a little income tax occasionally, if it made anybody happy.

During and since the days of the black market, he had been suspected of directing large-scale transport and dockyard robberies. Also a few crimes of violence had been unofficially set against his name, but there were three types of wrongdoing of which he had never for a moment been suspected by those who knew him. He detested the drug traffic, he detested blackmail, and he had never been any sort of pimp.

This dark-eyed and rather handsome man was physically formidable; of medium height, thickset and compact, quick and strong. Characteristically he flaunted his wealth. He was loud. His suit of fine worsted was pinkish-grey in colour. He wore diamonds on his fingers, in his tie, and in his cuff-links. His car was typical, a brand-new grey-and-white Rolls-Royce which stood out among the workaday cars at the kerb like a swan among ducklings.

Devery stopped beside the car. He grinned at it. "Hallo, Dixie," he said.

Dixie turned quickly, with a frown. Then the frown cleared. Nowadays he considered himself to be too great a man to converse with a common bogie, but with police officers of rank he still thought that affability was worth while. Devery was a detective of rank, recently acquired, as Dixie knew quite well. He made it his business to know all kinds of things about the police.

"Hallo, copper," he said with a smile. "What can I do for you?"

"I don't know, yet. Nice car you've got."

"Yes. Special body. I had to wait six months for it. I had to threaten to buy the place to make 'em get on with it."

Devery's grin widened. For all his years of affluence Dixie still had to brag like a barrow boy.

"Well," he conceded, "it certainly makes folk stare."

Dixie shrugged. "Let 'em stare. I couldn't care less about 'em staring. The proletariat! I got other things to think about."

"Such as?"

"This lark that's going on. This robbing and murdering. My pals in London are taking the mickey. The sceptre snatched from my feeble hand and all that sort of crap. They're making it out that this new mob is going to chase me out of town."

"They're well organized, Dixie," said Devery seriously.

"Well organized? A lot of flaming lunatics, if you ask me. They're bad for me, all the same. I can't afford to lose prestige. If this goes on, certain guys elsewhere will start to think they can take liberties with me. Then I shall have to get tough. It'll be like starting all over again."

"I'm sorry for you."

"It's all right laughing, but every newspaper in the country is busting out in headlines about Granchester. Three cold-blooded murders, for a start."

"Four. Wait till you've seen an evening paper."

Dixie stared. "Here, come and have a drink," he said. "Hell fire, I never loved a copper, but I'm on your side this time."

He turned to his car, and spoke to a gloriously over-dressed young woman who had been waiting to alight. "You stay there, Popsie," he said. "I got business. I'll send for you when I want you."

Devery followed the man into the main bar of the hotel. He looked at the broad back, and wondered. He did not trust Dixie as far as the first corner, but it seemed reasonable that Dixie would want to see an end of the terror which stalked in the city. It cocked a snook at his own shadowy authority, and the abnormal police activity which it had aroused was bad for any illegal business he had in mind.

"Hallo, Ella," said Dixie to the barmaid. And to Devery: "What's yours?"

"Just a glass of beer, please."

"Oh, have a short one. You're drinking with Dixie."

"No. Beer please. I'm supposed to be working."

"Well, so am I. I'm always working."

"Beer, please."

Dixie sighed humorously. "Have it your own way. Ella, a half of bitter and a double John Haig. And have something yourself."

"I'll have a drop of gin, Mr. Costello," said Ella.

When the drinks were served, Ella moved away, but not too far for her keen ears to pick up scraps of the talk.

"Now," said Dixie. "Who bought it this time?"

"Ewart Thompson. Do you know him?"

"I know him. A scruffy little tea-leaf. I didn't know he was a grasshopper, though."

"I don't think he was," said Devery. He gave Dixie an edited version of the incident at Elms House. As he listened, the tough mobster's expression revealed a certain amount of awe.

"What a shower," he commented when the story was told. "They don't stop at nothing, do they? Knocking off one of their own lot! Boy, that's chancy. There's no mob in the world will stand for that."

"I don't know about that. The Pl—— somebody seems to have them well trained."

"What's that you nearly said?"

"Nothing."

"Well, if it's nothing, tell me."

"No. It's not safe even for you to know. I couldn't tell you anyway."

"Not safe for me? You don't think *I'm* scared of 'em, do you? Why, if I could find out who they were I'd paralyse the lot of 'em. I'd butter the pavement with 'em."

"If they thought you were a danger to them, they'd do you before you knew who they were," said Devery.

Dixie stared. "My word, they might at that," he said, suddenly sobered. "I'd better stop shouting the odds." He was about to say something else in his strong speaking voice when he realized that the time to stop shouting the odds was *now*. "All the same, I'll smash 'em if I get half a chance," he mumbled confidentially.

"Who were Ewart Thompson's friends?" Devery wanted to know.

Dixie shook his head. Then in the same low voice he said: "I'll ask around."

"Thanks. And any jewellery deals, of course. Anything at all, in fact."

Dixie nodded. "But not a word to anybody."

"Not a word," Devery promised.

Dixie finished his whisky. Ella came to serve him again. Devery looked at her speculatively, wondering if she had been listening. She was a natural blonde, about thirty years of age. She was tall, with an excellent figure, and she moved in a graceful way. There was a thin scar down one side of her face, from ear to chin, and it pulled one side of her mouth slightly. The scar did not make her unattractive because her attraction was elemental, and men still looked at her with a glint in their eyes. Nevertheless, as she served another round of drinks, she kept her head turned a little to hide the scar. This attitude was habitual to her.

Devery, a bachelor and a decent fellow, had a sneaking regard for Ella. This liking was almost purely physical, and he knew it. He also knew that she was unsuitable company for him, a police officer. Still, when he was in her presence he was invariably tempted to try and achieve some sort of intimacy with her.

He knew the story of Ella's scar. Her husband, one Martin 'Caps' Bowie, had sliced her with a Kropp razor in drunken, baseless jealousy. He had gone to prison for that. Now she was legally separated from him, and there was an injunction to restrain him from approaching her or speaking to her. The evidence of her doctor had secured the injunction, on the grounds that she now had a pathological terror of Bowie. The very sight of him in the street was enough to send her running to the nearest policeman.

Bowie had indeed approached her on two occasions since his release from prison, sincerely attempting a reconciliation. But each time he had been drunk as well as sincere, and Ella had screamed at the sight of him. The first time, he had been turned away from Ella's flat and thrown down some stairs by well-meaning neighbours. The second time, still with the best of intentions, he had kept the neighbours at bay with his razor, an action which had naturally increased Ella's hysteria. The police had dealt with him on that occasion, and because his motive in showing the razor had been honestly misinterpreted by everyone, he had been given a further two months' cooling treatment at Farways prison. Since then he had stayed away from Ella.

"How are you, Ella?" Devery asked. Then he ventured: "Seen Caps lately?"

Ella shuddered and looked haughty. Dixie gave the

detective a swift, hard glance, because Caps Bowie was one of his 'boys', actually his own private tic-tac man and officially by profession a bookmaker's clerk.

"Don't mention Caps to Ella," he said with some severity. "She don't like it."

"Sorry, Ella," said Devery with false humility. "I didn't know it was as bad as that. I guess you'll be foot-loose and fancy free nowadays."

"You'd like to know, wouldn't you?" she retorted, somewhat mollified.

"Sure I'd like to know. When is your night off?"

"All my nights off are booked up, thank you."

"Just my bad luck. I'm too late again. Have I the honour of the young man's acquaintance?"

"No, and you won't have. He don't have no truck with the police. He's a gentleman."

"I'm glad. There are so few of us left. Has Caps heard of him?"

Ella's glance was enigmatic. There was mockery in her voice. "You want to know a lot, don't you? I'll tell you. My friend could break Caps up for firewood."

Devery's wide, crafty eyes reflected incredulity, and Dixie snorted.

"She's crackers," said Dixie with good-humoured scorn. "Why, I've seen Caps. . . . Caps is a very tough guy."

"He's not as tough as my friend," said Ella.

"Oh, to hell with Caps, and your friend an' all," said Dixie in disgust. "I didn't come in here to talk about them."

But Devery would not let the matter drop. Ella's little air of mystery intrigued him. And it appeared that she could, after all, listen to talk about her husband without turning pale.

"Have you got Caps under control?" he asked smoothly.

"Sure I've got him under control," Dixie retorted. "He works for me, don't he? Or didn't you know?"

"Yes, I knew. He's a slippery customer, isn't he?"

"Everybody in the racing game is slippery. What did Caps ever do to you? Why do you keep going on about him?"

Devery did not quite know himself. It was a feeling he

had, about Caps Bowie. Also, he never missed an opportunity of setting two rogues against each other.

"Caps never did me any harm," he said, as he rose from his bar stool. "Just you make sure he never does you any, Dixie boy."

CHAPTER FOUR

DEVERY returned to Headquarters with the intention of having a meal in the canteen. But first he looked into the C.I.D. office, and a clerk beckoned urgently.

"Just the man," he said, looking at the clock. "Somebody wants you on the phone. You and you alone. It was a female and she seemed to be in a state. You've got to ring her back at this number. She said she'd wait till one o'clock."

Devery looked at the number, Central 424011. The last two numerals meant that it was a public call box. Then he looked at the clock. The time was four minutes to one.

He dialled the number. The phone purred for a little while, and then someone picked up the receiver. Devery waited for the person to speak.

"Hallo. Who is that, please?" came the cautious question. It was not a woman who spoke. It was a man trying to sound like a woman. Also, there was the trace of an ineradicable accent. It was a Scotsman trying to sound like an English woman.

Devery looked thoughtfully at the clerk. The clerk was not a man who would be easily deceived. This, then, was not the original caller.

"Who is there?" the voice squeaked.

"I want Joe Liggins," said Devery, using the first name which came into his head. "That's Cleary's, isn't it? Put Joe on, will you?"

The Scotsman hung up, and Devery did likewise. He rang for a car. "You're quite sure it was a woman who rang?" he asked the clerk.

"Positive," was the reply. "A woman, and I'd say a young one."

"We have a list of call box numbers, haven't we? Where is this one situated?"

The clerk looked at the list. "The corner of Tyburn and Bishopsgate," he said. "Bang in the middle of town."

"Thanks," said Devery. He hurried out of the office.

A plain C.I.D. car had been brought round from the police garages. The garage man gave the number of the car as he handed it over, and Devery gravely repeated it. It was his business to return the car undamaged.

As he was starting the car, Devery descried Detective Constable Cook approaching at a jog trot. Cook was a burly young man; not extraordinarily bright, but patient and reliable. Devery called to him: "Are you very busy?"

Cook could scarcely spare the time to answer. "I'm on duty at one, sarge. I'll be late."

"Never mind. Get in the car. This job will clear you of being late. Step lively now!"

The car moved off as Cook scrambled into it. Devery drove as quickly as the traffic would allow in the direction of Tyburn Street. As he drove, he gave Cook the facts of the case.

"Do you think something has happened to the woman?" Cook wanted to know. "It looks as if somebody was watching her. Maybe they chased her away and then tried to take the call, to find out who she'd been talking to."

"That's about it. But they didn't get anything from me. But now we're going to that phone box. There's just a bare chance that we might see something."

Devery stopped the car some distance away from the call box. The street was busy with traffic and people. It was hard to tell if anyone was watching the box.

"I'll 'case' this side, you take the other," the sergeant said. "If you see any suspicious client, take note but do not disturb. If you want to give me the griff, show your hanky and blow your nose. Don't go near the box till you get the all clear from me."

They 'cased' the street. Neither man had occasion to

show his handkerchief. Nobody seemed to be watching, either from the street or through the window of a shop or restaurant. They met near the corner. Devery looked at the stout woman of forbidding countenance who was using the box at the moment.

"I'll bet that dame is giving her old man a rousting about something," he commented. "I hardly think she's the woman we want."

He went to the box and opened the door. The woman turned a stare of cold outrage upon him.

"Excuse me," he said, touching his hat. "Are you the lady who tried to phone the police station?"

"I certainly was not! How dare you interrupt a private. . . ."

Devery did not hear any more. He closed the door of the box and returned to his colleague.

"Now how could anybody have been molested at this corner, in the middle of the day?" he demanded. He stared around. Not far away there was a back street which ran behind shops. Anything could happen in a back street, at any time.

He led the way, satirically quoting a gem of Superintendent Clay's homespun wisdom as he went. "The way to find things is to look," he said.

The back street was deserted. On one side was the high rear wall of some sort of commercial building. On the other side were the tiny backyards of smart shops. The first yard had no gate. It was simply a place to keep rubbish bins.

"It's quiet enough here," he said, looking round intently. He stopped and picked up a very small brush.

"What's this?" he asked.

Cook examined the little article, less than half the length of his thumb. "It's one of those brushes women use to put black stuff on their eyelashes," he said with the superior knowledge of a married man. "My wife carries one about with her."

Devery nodded. He looked further, and so did Cook. In the narrow place between two of the bins the latter

33

found a small, gold-coloured cylinder. Even Devery knew what that was.

"Lipstick," he said. "Somebody searched a woman's handbag in here, and he wasn't too careful how he did it. It looks as if they had that woman in here. I wonder what they did with her."

Cook looked in the bins, turning over empty boxes and discarded wrapping paper. "Nothing here," he said.

They returned to the car, and Devery looked at his watch. It was still only eight minutes past one.

"Take the wheel," he said. "We'll cruise around a bit."

"Who are we looking for?" Cook wanted to know.

"I dunno," said Devery. "A damsel in distress, maybe."

They prowled in a wide circle, without much hope. But Devery's luck was proverbial. They were returning to their starting point when they saw the girl in Lacy Street. They both saw her, though the traffic was heavy and the sidewalks crowded.

She was hurrying along, in the opposite direction to the police car. Sauntering shoppers hindered her, but she pushed her way through in a frenzy to get to some place or away from some place. She held a handkerchief to her mouth. There was panic in her face, and she appeared to be sobbing. There was a bruise on her soft cheek which would undoubtedly develop into a black eye. Otherwise she was undeniably pretty and smart; a typist, or a worker of that class.

"That could be the bit of poultry we're looking for," said Devery. "Don't stop. Turn as soon as you can, and we'll see where she goes."

He looked at faces in the crowd of passers-by, but he did not see anyone he knew. But any one of half a dozen fast-walking men could have been following the girl.

The car reached a cross-roads, and Cook called to the policewoman on point duty. "I want to turn, Sunshine. Get me round."

The policewoman nodded, and stopped the traffic. As Cook was passing her she said: "Don't be so familiar, flat-foot." The Jaguar made a wide circle and just managed to get round. The policewoman said: "Drivers!"

"Now pick up the girl again," said Devery as the car gathered speed again. "Just keep her in sight."

The girl was now on the opposite side of the road, and she still had her following of men, if it was a following. She stopped at a pedestrian crossing, and waited for the lights to change. Cook also stopped, close to the kerb. Devery watched carefully. All the men who might have been following the girl went on up the street without glancing at her.

Then Devery's luck deserted him. The lights changed, and pedestrians crossed in a crowd. He watched the girl as she crossed. She looked at the Jaguar, and at him. He saw recognition in her face. He saw fear, too. Then she was over the crossing, and running. She ran straight through the nearest doorway of Woolworth's store.

Devery was out of the car in an instant. He ran to the doorway and entered the store, and found himself in a crowded, chattering world of women. He stood on his toes and looked out over a sea of feminine heads. There were hats of all colours, shapes, and sizes. There were hatless heads ranging in hue from black to platinum. The girl he sought was bareheaded, and her hair was of an indistinguished brown colour. In that crowd, he decided, he had not a cat-in-hell chance of picking her out. Still, he looked for her. He failed to find her. The store had seven main doorways, opening on to three busy streets.

He went back to the car. He and Cook cruised round the store and the adjacent streets for twenty minutes, but they did not see the girl.

They returned to Headquarters, and Devery told his story to Martineau, who had just entered his office.

"Hard luck," said Martineau. "You've got yourself a job now."

"How?"

"You'll have to find that girl. Obviously she knows you, though you don't know her. I imagine that she was going to tell you something over the phone, but she was under observation and she was stopped. Somebody walked her round the corner into the back street, searched her bag, knocked her about, and scared her silly. She won't talk now, but it might be helpful to know who she is. Are you quite sure you don't know her?"

"I've never set eyes on her before."

"Well, you'd better set eyes on her again. The way she's been treated indicates that she knows something important. She wasn't going to spill it to any old policeman, she wanted *you*. I'm hoping that what she knows has something to do with the Plumber."

"If she was a danger to the Plumber, why didn't he have her quietened for good, as he did with the other informers?"

"Well, I'm not kidding myself that he spared her because she was a woman. I'm inclined to assume that she is the wife or the sister of one of his boys. He knows that the police are very suspicious of sudden deaths these days, even if they look like accidents. If he killed the girl, subsequent police inquiries would bring her husband or her brother into the limelight. He doesn't want that."

"Tell me how I'm going to find her."

"It was during the lunch hour that she was trying to phone you, so you'd better work on the theory that she is employed somewhere in the centre of the town. She would be going back to the job when you saw her. You can start from that spot and work in the direction she was going."

"Will I have Cook to help me?"

"Of course."

"We'll have to nose around in a lot of places. If the Plumber is still keeping an eye on her, he might tumble to the idea. That might be very dangerous for the girl."

Martineau thought about that. He thought about it for quite some time.

"The Plumber *will* probably kill the girl if he finds out that we're looking for her," he said. "But it's unlikely that he'll find out. It's a chance we've got to take. You know the saying; you can't make an omelette without breaking a few eggs."

"There have been too many eggs broken already," said Devery bluntly. "I don't like it."

"Neither do I," was the reluctant answer. There was silence in the room.

"I'll tell you what," said Martineau at length. "You describe her as a worker of the better-dressed sort. Would you say she was the kind who might do a certain amount of shopping at Maxim's?"

"Yes, I'd say she might."

"Very well. A tremendous number of women in this town go into Maxim's at least once a week. Those who don't go to Maxim's go to Harrod's. You'll cover Maxim's and Cook will go to Harrod's. I'll fix it with the managements of both places for you to sit in the mezzanine. You're looking for a notorious shoplifter, we'll say. That'll get us all the co-operation we want."

Devery nodded. "We shall want walkie-talkie."

"Yes. Binoculars, radio, and a radio car waiting outside, so that she doesn't give you the slip again. It'll be a dull job with a lot of eyestrain. You'll have to be there whenever the store is open, because she might not work in a shop or an office. She might be a housewife who can appear at any time."

Again Devery nodded. "I'd sooner do it that way than risk being the cause of her getting what Willis Cooper got."

"Yes, it'll be safer. Anyway, that's how we'll do it. There's just a chance that it might lead us to something."

"Sure. How is everything else going?"

"Rotten. There isn't a whisper of anything. The town is sewed up."

"What about the car they used last night?"

"Found abandoned. It was a stolen car with false number plates. They left it on the car park near the United football ground. It's as clean as a whistle. Not even a thumb-print on the driving mirror."

"He's a character, the Plumber. He'll stop at nothing, and yet he's very careful."

"Yes. He knows just how and why thieves get caught after they've done a job. He allows no careless handling of anything. There's no blabbing and boasting, and no flash money. But he's bound to make a mistake sooner or later. We'll get him."

"You hope," said Devery.

"I fervently hope," Martineau rejoined rather wearily.

CHAPTER FIVE

WHEN Devery left him in the Northland Hotel, Dixie Costello sat frowning into his whisky glass.

"What's up with that cop?" he asked. "Keeping on about Caps like that?"

"He's a D, isn't he?" Ella the barmaid retorted without sympathy. "He knows his business. He doesn't ask questions without a reason. I wouldn't put anything past Caps Bowie, and whatever it is I hope the coppers get him for it."

"You're prejudiced, Ella," said Dixie. Then he added quickly: "Not that you haven't a right to be."

"When I see them putting a five-ton gravestone over him I'll be happy," said Ella, then she moved away along the bar.

Dixie was still contemplating his whisky when Ned Higgs entered the bar. Ned worked for Dixie, and could be described as his lieutenant or manager. When compelled to disclose his occupation he called himself a professional backer, and in a sense he told the truth. When Dixie couldn't be bothered to go to the races he sometimes sent Ned to wager his money for him.

Like his chief, Ned was of medium height, broad, strong, quick, nervy, and tough. He had to be tough to keep his place as Dixie's second-in-command.

"Hallo. You done Stepladder?" Dixie greeted him.

It was a reminder. Ned nodded and affirmed that he had wagered some money upon a racehorse called Stepladder.

"I was talking to Gus Hawkins," Ned went on. "He's laying it off. The price is shuttering."

"Never mind. It'll win," said Dixie with finality. "We'll get something."

"Sure," Ned agreed loyally. He was the only follower trusted by Dixie, and he was not trusted very far.

"Seen any of the boys this morning?" Dixie asked.

38

"I went to see Waddy. He's poorly, in bed with his back. A slipped disc, he calls it. I told him what it was."

Dixie lowered his voice. "Seen Caps at all?"

Ned was quick to notice a change of mood. He raised his eyebrows, and dropped his own voice. "Yes, I saw him, but not to speak to. Why, what's up?"

"Where did you see him?"

"Coming out of the Union Bank. He musta started saving up for his old age."

"H'm," said Dixie. Now he was definitely suspicious. He smelled treachery, but just what form the treachery was taking he had no idea. Caps Bowie was an inveterate gambler, and like most of his kind he invariably carried his total wealth in the buttoned-up fob pocket of his trousers. Now he was putting money in the bank, or taking it out. There was something very wrong somewhere.

"Did Caps see you?" Dixie asked.

"No, I don't think he did. I was on the other side of the street."

"Where did he go?"

Ned's eyebrows were higher than ever. "I never noticed where he went. What *is* this about Caps? Is there summat up?"

"I don't know. This is between you and me. I've just been talking to Devery, the detective. He was very nosy about Caps. He told *me* to watch my step with him."

"I'd better give Caps the tip-off, hadn't I?"

"No. We keep this squat, just the two of us. There's something funny going on. Caps going to the bank! I never heard of such a thing! We'll watch him, but he won't know it. See?"

"Okay, Dixie."

"And we'll be careful. These are funny times. There's been murders."

"Wow!" You don't think——"

"I don't think nothing. We'll be careful, that's all. I'm going to have some lunch now. Come on, I'll treat you."

"Thanks, Dixie. But what about your bit of stuff waiting outside?"

"Oh hell, I forgot about her," said Dixie, with an impatient snap of his fingers. "Go and bring her in, will you?"

* * * * *

When Dixie and his henchman had gone into the dining-room, Ella Bowie was left alone in the bar. It was the quiet part of the midday opening session, and she would probably have very few customers in the place before the three o'clock closing time. She had time to think.

She thought about men. She had long ago decided that they held their advantageous position in the world by brute strength, size and ferocity. They had all the money and they bossed you about and thought they were wonderful if they bought you a drink, and all the time they were as numb as trees. They couldn't see an inch in front of their noses: they didn't know what was going on. Even the police—another mob of big swaggering males—didn't know what was going on. They knew less than anybody. Neither their ears nor their eyes were sharp enough.

What she had guessed through listening and watching was extremely interesting. She perceived a trend of events which might have a gratifying result for her. She touched her scar when she thought of it. She was always conscious of the scar. It did not make her unattractive to men, she knew that. But it made her feel inferior to some other women. She was marred. She would never forgive Caps Bowie for the scar.

Neither did she want another scar, or an early funeral as a result of an 'accident'. It was all right for her to say that she hated the very sound of her husband's name; people expected that. But she must not let them think that she knew anything about his recent life, or that she gathered the tiniest scraps of information about him and fitted them together in her mind like pieces of a jigsaw puzzle. It was safe enough for Devery to throw out hints; he was a policeman. Devery was quite good-looking, she reflected. She wondered if he *really* knew anything about Caps. She thought that it might be a good idea to give him some encouragement, and let him talk. She

decided that she would give him the big smile the next time
he came into her bar.

*　　*　　*　　*　　*

At about that time Devery was settling down in a cell-
like chamber in a mezzanine which overlooked the ground
floor of Maxim's store. The tiny room had been made so that
a store security officer could sit there occasionally and watch
for shoplifters. It was equipped with two telephones—a
house line and a post office line—and now there was also
a portable field radio which the detective had brought with
him. He focused his binoculars and applied himself to his
work. He did not like that kind of work, but he realized that
the quickest way to get it done was to be on the alert for
every minute of the time he was there.

Having seen both Devery and Cook installed, Martineau
pursued his wearisome inquiries. In the evening, when
normally he would have been sitting in comfort at his own
fireside, he moved about in the centre of the city. In the
dead time between seven and nine, the early moderate
drinkers had gone home for the evening, and the late
moderate drinkers had not yet come out for the last hour
or so. Between seven and nine Martineau found the riff-raff,
the unfortunates, the mugs. He went in pubs, billiard saloons,
pubs, coffee bars, pubs, clubs of a sort, pubs, snack bars, pubs,
pubs, pubs. In those places he found the people who were
unhappy at home, uncomfortable at home, impatient, bored,
unwanted or lonely at home; those who were afraid to go
home and those who had no home. For such men and women
the pubs with warm fires, clean floors, bright lights and
companionable chatter were havens indeed. They were
places to live in, and homes were merely places to sleep.

Martineau liked a convivial pint of ale as much as any
man, but on his rounds, in these places, he drank sparingly.
He recognized many people for whom he felt mildly sorry,
he saw a number of people whom he knew to be dishonest
or morally reprehensible, he spotted a few whom he knew
to be criminals. Prostitutes looked at him with cold dislike,

41

bullies and hooligans looked the other way, pickpockets and sneak-in men touched their caps with nervous respect. He gave them all a cool smile and a nod.

At eight forty-five he walked into the Prodigal Son, and saw a look of guarded uneasiness come into Doug Savage's face.

"Now then, Doug," he said, when his half-pint of beer had been served. "How's business?"

"Shocking," said Doug. Then he added meaningly: "And getting worse."

Martineau grinned. "Hard times!" he sympathized. "Pub short of customers, or customers short of money?"

"Customers. Half of 'em daren't put their noses out of doors when the sun goes down. Your coming in here doesn't improve matters."

"I got that the first time. I'm just wondering if Ewart Thompson was in here lately."

"I couldn't tell you when I last saw Ewart," said Doug. "Who were his pals?"

"Eeh, I couldn't tell you. I doubt if he had any."

Martineau nodded. It was the sort of information he had been getting all day. He looked along the bar. There was Tom Egan, holding a pint of beer and staring at nothing, and obviously trying to listen. Martineau knew the man, and had a contempt for him: a big, swaggering bully, advertising the remains of a small reputation as a wrestler by going about in a gaudy sweater. Why couldn't the fellow dress like other people?

Egan had a record. He had served one or two short prison sentences for small, mean crimes. Martineau remembered that. He looked hard at Egan, taking in every detail of the man's appearance. The ex-bruiser immediately became aware of the glance, but he did not return it. He swore quietly in a disgusted sort of way, as if to himself. Then he drank off his beer and walked out of the inn.

There was nothing in Egan's action to arouse suspicion. Indeed, at a time when people of that type were afraid to be seen talking to a policeman, it was a natural thing to do. Martineau was not suspicious. He drank up his own beer and followed Egan because he had suddenly decided to call it a day and go home.

But he turned at the door, to say good night to Doug, and he surprised a look of wild surmise on that cagey young man's face which made him ponder. He still pondered as he watched the meaty shoulders, fat neck, and bullet head of Egan moving along Tyburn Street. He warned himself that Doug's quickly hooded stare might mean nothing at all. He also told himself that you go to work on nothing when you have nothing to work on. He followed the striped jersey.

Egan turned the corner into Lacy Street, and as he turned he looked back and raked Tyburn Street with a deliberate glance. Obviously he saw Martineau under the bright overhead lights. Martineau walked on steadily, Egan went round the corner.

Martineau did not pause to consider how it would profit him to persist in following a man who had become aware of his presence. He just went on behind Egan, walking steadily. There were not many pedestrians about at that time in the evening, because the shops were closed and the public houses, cafés and cinemas were still open. Concealment from Egan, if he turned to look, was impossible. But as yet he could not be sure whether Martineau was following him or merely walking in the same direction.

Egan came opposite the long, high frontage of Maxim's store, whose big windows were, oddly enough, in darkness. He stopped at the corner of Queen Street, and lit a cigarette. Then he stood for a few seconds pensively holding the burning match in his fingers. He did not turn his head to right or left, but dropped the spent match and went on his way.

Martineau followed, and when he reached Queen Street he looked about him. He saw a man pull his head back into a doorway just along Queen Street, on the near side. Egan could not have seen this man unless he had had eyes in his ears, because he definitely had not turned his head.

Martineau also looked the other way, across the road to Maxim's arcade, which was a haunt of giddy young girls and young men, and prostitutes and their prospective

43

customers. It was also, normally, very well policed, because there had been a number of complaints from respectable citizens who had been accosted therein. The arcade was adequately lit by overhead lamps, but they were not so brilliant as the sodium lights of the street, and there was an effect of gloom. Martineau looked that way, and wished that he had looked a second or two sooner. Somebody was running in the arcade, or rather running out of it at the other end; a man who was too far away and too briefly glimpsed to be recognized.

So there was Egan walking ahead, and a man lurking in the nearby doorway, and another man running away with a hundred yards' start, and none of them might have any connexion with another. But Egan's business with the cigarette and the match had looked uncommonly like a signal of some sort, and the man in the doorway had pulled in his head too quickly for it to be an ordinary sort of movement. Martineau went along to the doorway.

The man there was Ned Higgs, whom he knew to be an associate of Dixie Costello. "Evening, Inspector," said Higgs affably, when they came face to face.

"Good evening, Ned," said Martineau. "What are you doing here?"

"I was supposed to meet a tart here, but it looks as if she's made a mug of me," was the unhesitating reply. "I've been waiting twenty minutes."

That, Martineau reflected, was a falsehood. Higgs would not meet a girl out in the street while places of refreshment were open. Or if he did, he was unlikely to wait twenty minutes for her. He would go away and have a drink, and return.

But Martineau did not give Higgs the lie. "Happen she doesn't like you as much as you thought," he said genially. "Who was that fellow running out of the other end of the arcade?"

Higgs leaned out of the doorway and looked towards the arcade. "I dunno, Inspector," he said. "Was there somebody running?" His expression and his voice were only a little too innocent. His interest in the fact of a man running was only slightly exaggerated. He was a good liar and nearly a good actor.

"All right, Ned. I hope you're not disappointed," said Martineau. "Good night to you."

"Good night, Inspector," Higgs replied, very respectful and friendly.

Martineau went on his way. He could have 'turned up' Higgs for firearms or offensive weapons. Dissatisfied with the man's answers as he was, he could have taken him to Headquarters and questioned him harshly and persistently. Either of these actions would probably have been a waste of time. It was better to let Higgs be of the opinion that he had got away with it, whatever it was.

Now, Egan was out of sight, and the policeman guessed that he had turned the first corner and walked along Union Street, where Willis Cooper had so recently met his fate. But in Union Street there was no sign of Egan. Martineau walked along the street to the first crossroads, and back along the other side. There was a tavern on the other side. He looked into the saloon bar. Egan was there, alone at the bar. Martineau quietly closed the tavern door and went to Headquarters. At Headquarters there was nothing new, so he went home. He was of the opinion that the Plumber's gang would not be doing a job that night.

CHAPTER SIX

MARTINEAU went on duty the following morning, and learned with a special sort of satisfaction that the Plumber and his men had not been in action during the previous night.

"Of course they don't do a job every night," said Superintendent Clay. "They've got to pick their spots, spy out the land, and get organized."

"They did three jobs in three nights, last week," said Martineau, who sometimes felt impelled to argue with Clay even when argument was futile.

"That is so, but they can't keep it up."

"They might lay off for a while now," Martineau rejoined, half in agreement. He thought that last night he might have disturbed the gang, or upset some arrangement. He did not mention that to Clay. There was nothing to tell, really. And in any case, Clay's reaction would be to ask questions of the "Why didn't you do this" or "Why didn't you do that" variety. Clay was a good policeman, and a good-natured man up to a point, but he had the common fault of superior officers. *After* the event he could not refrain from telling his subordinates what *should* have been done.

Martineau went to his own office. He telephoned his two watchers at Maxim's and Harrod's, and learned that they had nothing to report. Then he picked up a pencil and began to scribble names.

Tom Egan. Egan was the sort of tearaway who could be expected to gravitate naturally to a race gang, but he had never been known to have dealings with Costello or any of his mob. Come to think of it, that was strange. Besides being a petty thief and a rowdy, Egan was a gambler and an associate of gamblers. He followed the horses and occasionally went to the races. He frequented the gaming schools. He went to greyhound tracks. He must have met Costello many a time, and of course he knew him because all of his kind knew Costello. There had been times in the past when Costello needed as many men of Egan's type as he could recruit, but he had never recruited Egan. Now, when Dixie was able to settle gang disputes without bloodshed, he had hardly enough work for his regular boys. So, did it look as if the gang leader was now employing Egan in some capacity? It did not.

And yet Martineau felt sure that there had been something afoot last night which he, Martineau, had caused to be postponed or abandoned. There had been men on both sides of Lacy Street. One man, possibly more than one, possibly half a dozen, had beat a retreat when Egan had stopped on the corner and illuminated his own face with a match. Another man, in a doorway, had thought it better to stay where he was. Ned Higgs, Dixie Costello's right hand.

Thinking about Higgs, Martineau realized that he might be making a mistake in assuming that the Plumber's crowd was the only active gang of thieves in the city. Himself and the entire force could think of nobody but the Plumber these days, and they could be wrong. Dixie's men might have been on some ploy of their own, which had nothing to do with the Plumber. They might have been on some business which had nothing to do with Dixie, either. Was that likely? It was not. Ned Higgs was far too cautious and sensible to work behind Dixie's back at a time when abnormal police vigilance was an embarrassment to every crook in the city. It was fairly safe to assume that whatever Higgs had been doing, he had been doing it for Dixie.

Was Dixie the Plumber, or in league with the Plumber? Martineau thought seriously about that. He knew Dixie of old. He knew him far better than Devery did. He knew that Dixie could be utterly ruthless. To Martineau's knowledge, he had maimed a number of men. If he were pushed to it, he would kill without hesitation.

Had the killer of Allott, Straw, Cooper and Thompson been pushed to it? In a sense he had. He would consider that he was amply justified. He had acted in self-protection.

So Dixie *could* be the murderer, or the man responsible for the murders. That seemed slightly incredible, but only because it showed Dixie in a new light: not a man who killed in the heat of a gang fight, but one who killed by order, after some thought. A real gangster, in fact.

Martineau reflected that Dixie would now have been told about his encounter with Higgs last night, so there could be no harm in talking to him about it. He looked up the telephone number and dialled it. Costello himself answered the call.

"Martineau here," the policeman said. "I want to talk to you, Dixie."

"Well, you know where I live."

"I'll see you here, at Headquarters."

"Oh, be damned to you. You can't boss me about."

"I want to see you here. If you won't come, I'll send somebody to fetch you."

"You can't do that. I've done nothing."

"I'll do it, anyway."

"Oh, all right, blast you. I'll come. What's it all about?"

"This and that."

"Is it about seeing Ned Higgs last night?"

That seemed to be a forthright question which might lead to a satisfactory explanation. "Yes, it's partly about that," Martineau admitted.

"Well, he lied to you. He wasn't waiting for any wench. He was doing a confidential job for me. There was nothing illegal about it. Nothing for you to bother about."

"There seemed to be plenty for me to bother about. I saw one fellow running like a hare."

There was no reply from Dixie.

"Who was it?" Martineau asked sharply.

"How would I know?"

"Because Higgs knows. I'm damn sure he knows."

Dixie became persuasive. "Look, Inspector. Just trust me a little way in this, will you?"

'Like hell I'll trust you,' Martineau thought. But he listened.

"I'm on your side in this job. I'm as anxious as you are to stop this swine who's doing all the robbing and murdering. I'm against him. The bloody man's not civilized."

Uttered by Dixie, the last remark held a certain amount of wry humour for Martineau. His voice softened a little.

"You spoke in the singular," he said.

Dixie was startled. "I did what?"

"When you mentioned robbing and murdering you referred to one single person. Do you know who that is?"

"Hell, no! I wish I did. If I knew, I'd tell you. Word of honour I would."

"Then why don't you give me some information now?"

"I've none to give you, but I will have. When I get results, I'll tell you."

"Where does Tom Egan come into it?"

"I don't know. But you can take it from me he's in something. He'll bear watching."

'So,' thought Martineau, 'Now we know that Egan isn't Dixie's man. He doesn't care what happens to Egan.'

"You're not giving anything away, Dixie," he said.

"I aren't, am I? But I will, Inspector, I will. I'm with you on this, but for God's sake not a word to anybody. If it gets out that I'm co-operating with the police I'll be ruined. There's only you, me and Higgs knows about this. We'd better keep it that way."

"That's the way we'll keep it, Dixie."

"Okay, Inspector. Now do you still want me to come over there and talk?"

"No, we'll leave it. But keep in touch."

"I will. You can trust me, Inspector."

'About as far as I'd trust a starving leopard,' said Martineau to himself as he put down the telephone. Having learned little from Dixie, he returned doggedly to his routine inquiries, following them into blind alleys and dead ends, and returning patiently to his starting point, and beginning afresh. Two nights later there was a hotel burglary involving the jewels of a visiting film star. The burglary was completely successful, despite police precautions. The film star saw nobody, but the crime was automatically put on the Plumber's list. With a film star in the business, the newspaper headlines were bigger than ever. The Chief Constable visited his doctor. It appeared that he was troubled by a gastric ulcer.

One thing was certain. Tom Egan took no part in the hotel burglary. He was under observation all the time, and no doubt he knew it. So, of course, the Plumber would know it if Egan was the Plumber's man. No doubt Egan had been given indefinite leave of absence from night work. Still, the police continued to watch him. They were clutching at straws.

Then, on Saturday afternoon, a little more progress was made. Devery saw the girl with the black eye in Maxim's store. She went upstairs on the escalator, and he waited anxiously for her return. While he waited, he phoned for Cook to come over from Harrod's. He posted him at the only exit which he could not see himself, and then he waited. Half an hour later he saw her come downstairs and make for one of the main entrances. He warned his colleagues who waited outside in a car, and then he ran. The car was able to get into the traffic of Lacy Street and pick him up while he still had the girl in sight.

"All right," he said comfortably, as he settled down in the back seat of the car. "Just tail along after her and don't get too near." He lit a cigarette and relaxed. In the rear seat he had enough room to get down out of sight if some accident of the chase brought the girl near enough to recognize him.

The girl caught a bus in Somerset Square and alighted in Shirwell, an inner suburb of faded gentility which was still mainly inhabited by its original settlers or their relicts. There was a local saying about Shirwell, 'evening dress and no dinner', which seemed to caricature its pretensions adequately enough. The girl entered a neat, small house in a quiet street of similar houses, and the police drove past and noted the address: Number 17 Larch Street.

Devery had spent a lot of time waiting for the girl, and he was prepared to spend a little more to be sure of her. The police car waited for three hours, with a man watching the back of the house, and the girl did not emerge.

"It looks as if we've seen her home," said Devery. "We'll leave her for a bit. Let's get back to town and have some tea."

At Headquarters, consultation of the Burgess Roll revealed that 17 Larch Street was occupied by a family called Blundell. A brief search of the local police records revealed the name of Owen Blundell, 17 Larch Street, who had served a sentence of twelve months imprisonment for falsification of accounts.

"Just another lad who got the firm's money mixed up with his own," Devery commented when he saw the card.

Owen Blundell had served his sentence at Granchester Prison, better known as Farways, and he had been released some four months ago. As he considered that, Devery began to look thoughtful. But he made no comment in the presence of the records clerk. Like any other decently ambitious man, he made a habit of expressing his bright ideas where they would do him the most good, instead of airing them as soon as he thought of them and letting some sharper opportunist run to knock at the inspector's door. He wanted the inspector to have his ideas before they became common knowledge. If the inspector passed them on to the superintendent, and took credit for them himself—well, that was human nature. That was just one of the crosses an underling had to bear.

He also had another reason for remaining silent. He did not want to be in any way responsible for another murder. If any police officer talked out of turn, it was not going to be Detective Sergeant Devery.

He got out the crime report relating to Owen Blundell's offence, and when he read it he remembered that he had been in court when the young man was tried. He remembered him; tallish, slight, fair-haired, pale-faced, handsome in a weak or boyish sort of way. A typical embezzler, he thought. He waited until Martineau returned from one of his inquiries, and followed him into his office. The chief inspector threw his hat on to a hook and sank wearily into his desk chair. "You've found the girl, then?" he asked without enthusiasm.

"Yes," Devery replied briskly. "I followed her home. Larch Street, in Shirwell. The name appears to be Blundell. There is an Owen Blundell of that address who is on our books."

"For what?"

"Embezzlement."

"Let me see," said Martineau. He took the report, with its attached statements, and read it. Owen Blundell, twenty-three years old at the time of the offence, had been employed as a general clerk by a small firm of brass founders. He had worked in the foundry office for five years, and he had had the run of the place. He had abused his employer's trust by falsifying his accounts of wages paid, taking two or three pounds for himself each week over a period. He might have gone on like that for a very long time, but his employer got at loggerheads with the Commissioners of Inland Revenue. The subsequent examination of books revealed the system of defalcation. Blundell was sent for trial. He pleaded guilty, and was sent to prison.

Devery handed over the record card, and Martineau looked at the photograph.

"A miserable sort of crook," he commented. "A dog who'll bite the hand that feeds him.'

"Not necessarily," was Devery's tolerant reply. "Maybe he's just a weak kid who couldn't resist temptation."

"Pah! I'd sooner have an honest cut-throat."

"He might be a cut-throat, now. You know what prison can do to some of the young ones."

"Oh, possibly, possibly. But this one looks like a softie to me."

"He might be a softie who can climb where nobody else can climb, or clear a jeweller's window like a conjurer. Or he may just be some sort of a crook's errand boy. We'll have to be careful. If he's one of the gang, and the Plumber finds out we're wise to him, he'll blame it on the girl."

"That's true. We don't want anything to happen to her. But we'll have to sit on the tail of this Owen Blundell."

"That may not be necessary, sir," said Devery carefully, because this was the moment to bring out his idea.

"Why not?" his superior officer demanded.

"A few discreet inquiries at Farways might take us beyond Blundell. He can only be small fry. We want the king fish."

"What do you mean? Why Farways?"

"Blundell came out of Farways in June. Tom Egan came out of there in March. Ewart Thompson was in there not so long ago. So were George Allott and Tommy Straw, with short sentences. Willis Cooper came out last November, nearly a year ago."

Martineau was excited now. His grey eyes glinted. "You think this gang was started in prison?"

"It could have been," said Devery calmly.

Martineau struck his left palm with his right fist. "If it was, we have the name of the Plumber on our books!"

"If he's a local man. we have."

"And if he isn't local, the prison authorities will have his name. He must be some man who was released from Farways within the last few months."

Devery had had more time to think about the matter. *"Was* he released?" he asked softly.

Martineau frowned. "You mean Beadle, Sayers and Carew? You think he could be one of those?"

"Well, they've never been caught, have they?"

Thoughtfully the chief inspector shook his head. Three men had escaped from Farways about four months ago. That was a remarkable feat, because Farways was a very 'tight' prison. But it was not unique. The unique thing was that none of the escapers had been recaptured.

"A peterman, a burglar, and a racing driver gone wrong," said Martineau. "None of them local men."

"No, but they could be hiding locally."

"You think one of them could be the Plumber?"

"I don't have an idea about that. But the Plumber could certainly use *all* of them."

"I guess he could. I'm going to have the names of all the men who came out of Farways during the past twelve months. I'm going to trace them all."

"Discreetly, of course, sir."

Martineau grinned suddenly. "I'm always discreet, aren't I? My word, Devery, you may have done yourself a bit of good today. The man who is the means of clearing up this little lot will find promotion staring him in the face."

"We can all do with a bit of that, sir. What's the first move?"

"The first move is for you to button your mouth. Have you mentioned this to anybody?"

"No, sir. Nobody at all."

"As if you would! Now then, only you and I, Superintendent Clay and the Chief need to know about it. Clay will have to get the information from Farways, in such a way that there can be no leak at that end as to what we're after. I'll go and have a word with Clay now. As a preliminary move, you go and get the record cards and bring them in here."

"What, all of them?"

"The lot," said Martineau, as he rose from his chair.

CHAPTER SEVEN

At 12.35 a.m. on Friday the 28th of September the caretaker of the Northern Counties Bank building in Granchester fell out of bed. His head thumped the floor and there was a dull noise in his ears. He sat up, confused and only half awake.

"What was that?" asked his wife from the bed.

"It was me," he said angrily, because his wife was a large, warm woman and a snuggler, and he habitually slept on the extreme edge of the bed to escape her suffocating embrace.

"It was a sort of thud," she said.

"It was my head hittin' the floor. I wish you'd stop in your own half of the bed."

"It shook the building."

"It shook me, an' all," said the caretaker, getting back into bed. "Move over! You don't leave enough room for a cat."

"It was a proper bang."

"I know it was," the caretaker retorted crossly. "My head is still ringin'. I'll have a lump like a hen-egg tomorrer. Get over on your own side and go to sleep!"

The explosion in the bank five floors below, which had made the caretaker roll from his precarious perch, had been heard by a constable and a sergeant who were a few hundred yards along the street. They were both on temporary plain clothes duty, and they had met quite by accident. They stood there in the middle of the richest part of the city, and looked at each other.

"What was that?" the P.C. wanted to know.

"*Where* was it?" the sergeant demanded.

"That way, I'd say. Could it have been a backfire?"

"Backfire? God help you, somebody's blown a safe. But where?"

The sergeant stared in perplexity along the street. Within a stone's throw there were five banks. There were also shipping offices, airline offices, insurance offices, advertising

54

offices, prosperous shops and stores, and the premises of exporters, importers, stockbrokers, and merchants of many kinds. There was an awful lot of money about.

"Go along and look," he said. "I'll follow you when I've rung in."

The P.C. padded away along the street, and the sergeant ran fifty yards in the other direction, to a police telephone box. He passed on his news and views to Headquarters, and as he turned away from the box its red signal light began to wink in-out-in-out.

He was only a few yards away from the box when he heard another sound. He stood still to listen. He could hear a car, but even in the clear, quiet night air the sound was faint. The car was purring along and making little noise, or else it was some distance away. Very soon the sound died away altogether. The sergeant returned to the box and phoned his additional news to the communications room.

Now, all over the city, the lurking plain-clothes men were 'ringing in' in answer to the winking lights. They were receiving the sergeant's message and beginning to close in to his assistance. Further out, area patrol cars were moving in after their crews had received the message by radio. Within minutes, the sergeant hoped, there would be an adequate cordon around the area in which the explosion had occurred.

He set off once more to find the constable, not risking either a flash of his torch or a low whistle, in case he might also advertise his presence to some thieves' look-out. He moved along very quietly, and soon he met the P.C. as the latter came running a-tiptoe out of a little street in which the Northern Counties Bank had a side door.

Glaring with excitement, the P.C. grasped his arm. "It's the bank!" he hissed. "They're in there! We've got 'em!"

During his service, the sergeant had seen many promising situations turn out to be heart-breaking false alarms.

"Have you heard 'em inside?" he asked.

"No. But the side door is bust open. They can't have come out yet."

The sergeant went to the door. It was standing ajar.

Holes had been bored near the top and bottom, and the two bolts had been expertly drawn, probably with thin copper wire. In addition, the strong lock looked as if it had been cracked by an outsize jemmy. The sergeant was a courageous man, but he was also discreet. He did not think that it would do any good for himself and the constable to go in there and meet four or five armed bank robbers.

He stationed the P.C. at the rear corner of the bank, and he went to the front corner. By this arrangement they could watch the three open sides of the building and have the open door in plain sight between them. They were in that position a minute or two later when the first of the reinforcements arrived. This was a plain-clothes man on foot. The sergeant sent him to join the other constable at the rear.

Then a car arrived, and it was followed by a police van carrying the ten men of the emergency squad. In the car was the duty inspector for the division. The sergeant explained the situation to him.

"All right," said the inspector. "If they're in, they'll know we're here by now. They might go up to the roof and try that sort of getaway. I'll have the whole block surrounded."

He gave the necessary orders to the sergeant in charge of the squad, who were armed with Enfield ·45 revolvers. Then he went into the bank. With him were the sergeant and constable who had made the discovery, and two of the armed squad men.

The way was through a lobby into the main hall of the bank. There was a strong reek of explosive, and a thin veil of smoke hung in the still air. The beam of the sergeant's torch came to rest on a main switchboard, and he put on the lights. The whole of the ground floor was quickly searched, and the entrance to the vaults was found. The iron door at the head of the vault stairs had been blown. It was hanging open.

The inspector led the way down the stairs, switching on the lights as he went. The party was confronted by a modern strong-room door which looked as if it would have withstood the discharge of an atomic cannon. There was no sign of disorder.

"They saw that door and didn't even try to blow it," the inspector said to the sergeant. "They cleared off straight away. That was the car you heard."

The sergeant was doubtful. He went back to the door at the head of the stairs. Though it was a steel door, it had only one ordinary mortise lock.

"Why did they waste their soup on this?" he queried. "They could have forced it the same way as they forced the street door."

The inspector became thoughtful. He was still pondering when the sergeant suddenly exclaimed: "It's a plant, same as that fire! They broke in and made a big bang to draw every policeman in town here! They'll be doing a job somewhere else!"

"My word!" said the inspector, with some apprehension as his own responsibility for the affair became evident to him. "You could be right." He paused only for a moment before he spoke again. "Anyway, there's nothing here. We'll leave two men on guard, and get the rest of them back to their beats. It's to be hoped we won't be too late."

He went out, shouting orders. The sergeant detailed the two armed men to remain in the bank, and then he also went outside. He now had only one idea, about one kind of shop. When he reached the corner where the police car stood, he found that the inspector's thoughts were moving in the same groove.

"Get round all your jewellers," he was urging the men as they came up. By radio he passed on his order to Headquarters, and to the listening cars of the area patrols. Then he got into his own car, and the sergeant got in with him.

"We'll try the far side of Lacy Street," the inspector said to the driver. The car shot away, and its tyres squealed on the dry tarmac as it took the first corner.

The occupants of the police car were only too late by a few seconds. When they had driven for half a mile up Lacy Street, shining their torches on the fronts of shops and looking along side streets, they went along Charlotte Street and returned by Padgham Hill. From Padgham Hill, looking along All Saints Road, they saw in the lamplit distance a three-ton lorry standing with its rear wheels on the sidewalk. It was backed up against the doorway of a jeweller's shop.

The driver of the lorry saw the police car immediately. He put his finger on his horn button and kept it there for several seconds. The group of men working feverishly at the rear end of the lorry seemed to break up. The men swooping down in the police car saw individual figures more clearly as men scrambled on to the lorry. They saw the lorry begin to move.

The lorry turned as it moved, but it moved at a speed too great for the available manœuvring space in that narrow street. While the last man was still scrambling aboard, its offside wheels mounted the opposite kerb, then jolted off as the lorry roared away along the street. The jolt came at the moment when the last man was pulling himself on to the lorry. His accomplices who had been helping him had decided that he was safe, and they had ceased to hold him. They had let go just a fraction of a second too soon. The lorry shrugged him off when its rear offside wheel dropped back into the roadway. He fell into the road, and into the path of the oncoming police car.

There was not much room to swerve, and practically no time to think. But the police driver did swerve, probably from sheer involuntary reaction. The man in the road rolled to avoid the car, and rolled straight into its path. The car went over him, and stopped.

"Get out and see to that man, Sergeant," the inspector ordered. The sergeant got out, and the car went on after the lorry.

The inspector gave out his position and direction on the radio. He described the lorry as best he could. The operator at Headquarters began to instruct other cars in a converging movement.

The car quickly overhauled the lorry, though the bigger vehicle was being driven expertly, at a dangerous speed. "Just stay on his heels until something gets in his way," the inspector ordered. "We can't run a three-tonner off the road with this car." He peered ahead through the windscreen. "It looks as if they've got the safe," he said. "Took the safe out of the shop, the cheeky devils."

Another police car came racing up from the rear, making a procession of three vehicles. This encouraged the inspector's driver to draw nearer to the lorry, in a narrow street. It was a mistake. Someone on the lorry began to shoot, and the front tyre of the car burst. It veered wildly, and hit a lamp post, and skated to a stop, blocking the road. The second car managed to stop without crashing into it.

The inspector got out and ran to the undamaged car, and climbed in. "Get on!" he urged. "Get after them!"

The driver quietly answered "Yes, sir," to the unnecessary order. He had to back off, and then manœuvre the long Jaguar on to the pavement to get by. The lorry was out of sight. It had turned a corner, and at the next cross-street there was no sign of it. The inspector erroneously concluded that because the driver of the lorry had been going in a certain direction, then it was the direction he wanted to go. "Try Sale Street," he said, and acting under orders the driver went the wrong way.

The driver of the lorry took full advantage of the mishap to the police car. He guessed that police cars would be closing in on him from all directions, and he also guessed that with two of the cars held up in a narrow street there was now a hole in the net. Having turned left, he turned left again, doubling back on his former route. He was out of the net.

Having been chased in the wrong direction in the first place, he was now able to get on to the getaway route which had been carefully planned for him. He had been driven over it several times, so that he would not make a mistake in the dark. The way had been chosen for its good surface, so that the lorry would make little noise; for its lack of shops and lock-up property, so that there would be an absence of policemen; for the respectability and also the poverty of its inhabitants, so that there would again be no policemen; for the fact that they were not main streets or short cuts, so that there was little chance of meeting other vehicles late at night. It was a twisting and tedious route, and it would have been difficult for anyone who saw the lorry to predict its general direction. It crossed only two main streets, and when it had crossed the second one it was in Darktown.

Darktown was the local name for an area which was covered by half a hundred little streets, all more or less alike, comprising rows and rows of brick dwelling-houses all built pretty much on the same pattern. This 'estate', built at the turn of the century and given the flattering name of Arcadia, had lately been infiltrated by coloured immigrants, mainly Jamaicans and Nigerians, who had caused the place to be given its new name. The streets were still gas-lit at night, and to a stranger they were only distinguishable one from another by the occasional small corner shops and the few small public houses. Here again the police did not come, except to deal with disturbances when the pubs were closing. At a time when the police were abnormally busy protecting valuable property, a policeman was not to be expected in Darktown at all.

The lorry turned this way and that among the streets, still being driven along the ones where the surface was least likely to cause noise. After travelling some distance in this way the driver came to a street which was distinguished by having a shabby little inn in the middle of the block.

"This is it," said the man who sat beside him. He stopped the lorry, and reversed it into the passage which led to the backyard of the inn. The yard was a cobbled space surrounded by old stables which were now let off as workshops to carpenters and other small tradesmen. It was not overlooked by any windows except those of the inn. In the yard it was almost totally dark, but no one showed a light.

The back door of the inn was opened, and a man came out. "All clear," he announced in a hoarse whisper. "No bobbies stirring. I've been watching for an hour."

The man who had been sitting beside the driver briefly murmured a reply, and then he said: "Get on with it." The innkeeper opened a double-leaf trapdoor near the back door. Beneath the trapdoor there was a chute which was normally used for getting barrels of beer down into the cellar. Everyone except the man who had given the order joined in quietly lifting the safe off the lorry, manhandling it to the cellar entrance and, with a rope, letting it slide gently down the chute. Then all the men except the driver and the inn-keeper went down the chute by the narrow steps cut in the middle of it. The last of these men, who were four in number, stopped to bolt the trapdoor after it had been closed from outside.

The innkeeper went indoors, locking the door behind him. He did not go to bed, but resumed his watch from a darkened room. He did not want to have anyone listening around while men were working on a safe in his cellar.

Only the driver was left. He got into the lorry and drove it away, and left it in a dead end half a mile away. He saw no policeman, because he still followed a pre-arranged route. When he left the lorry he did not need to wipe off any finger-prints. There would be no trouble about prints. Everyone had worn gloves.

He walked home, a matter of a few hundred yards. He was nervous and careful, because when he was on foot in the streets he was out of his element. He stopped at every corner and looked every way. And when he got home he stood motionless for several minutes in the doorway, peering along the lamplit street and listening. When he got out his key and entered, he was quite certain he had not been followed.

He went to bed without putting on a light, so careful was he. Those were the Plumber's explicit orders. and he could see the sense of them. But when he was in bed he lit a badly-needed cigarette, and inhaled luxuriously. He was tired, worn out by strain, but he was not sleepy. As he smoked and stared up into the darkness he wondered how long his mates would be before they got the safe open. He also thought about his pal Sayers who, apparently, had fallen off the lorry during the getaway. Probably the police had got Sayers. Too bad. He would go back to Farways for years and years.

The man in bed was not greatly concerned. Sayers would never sing to the police. Not one word. Never.

* * * * *

Sayers could not sing, because he was dead. The heavy three-and-a-half litre police car had injured him so seriously that he had died on the way to hospital. He had died without saying a word, but his very presence at the scene of the crime made the police reasonably certain that Beadle, Sayers and Carew, the three escaped convicts, had been hiding in or near Granchester for months. They had been skulking almost in the shadow of the prison which had failed to hold them. It could be assumed that Beadle the safe-blower and Carew the racing driver were still active members of the Plumber's gang.

The jeweller's shop was a heartrending sight for the Chief Constable when he arrived. The thieves had practically emptied it of valuables. The windows, showcases and drawers had been cleared of watches and jewels. The more valuable gems had been locked up in the safe for the night, but the safe had been taken. Only the more bulky or fragile articles such as clocks and cut glass had been left behind. The value of the stolen property, when computed, would undoubtedly add up to many thousands of pounds.

The means of entry had been simple and ingenious. The gang had stolen their lorry from a garage in a builder's yard, and from the yard they had also stolen a long plank. When laid on the platform of the lorry, the plank had protruded some six feet beyond the lowered tailboard. It had been used as a battering ram. Outside the jeweller's shop the lorry, expertly aligned, had been reversed so that the end of the plank hit, first, the lock of the metal grille guarding the doorway, and, second, the lock of the door itself. Neither of the strong locks had been able to withstand the shock of the three-tonner's assault.

It had been a quick but noisy entry, but noise had not been an important factor of the operation. The shop had been carefully chosen for a raid of that sort. It was in a street of lock-up premises with only one resident. The resident was Dixie Costello, who lived in a flat over a small restaurant which he owned. Apparently the Plumber had been well aware of Dixie's habitation. The telephone wires had been cut, and the door of the flat had been made immovable by screwing an ordinary hinge to the outside, fastening the door to the jamb. With the police lured away and Costello immobilized merely as a precaution, the raiders had been able to make a reasonable amount of noise with impunity.

Dixie had seen something of the operation from his bedroom window, about a hundred and fifty yards away from the jeweller's shop. He had been too far away to recognize anyone, but he had counted five men, excluding the driver of the lorry. There had also been another witness, but she refused to admit that she had seen anything at all. This was the young woman called Popsie, who was temporarily living on the fat of the land and calling herself Mrs. Costello. She said that she had slept through everything. The current Mrs. Costello wanted no publicity.

Dixie was furious. For some reason he appeared to regard the bold and well-planned raid as an insult to himself. He picked up a table-lamp and smashed it by throwing it on the floor. He stamped on a hat for which Popsie had just incurred a bill of fifteen guineas. He mentioned, in detail, what he was going to do to this impudent mob when he got his hands on them. He was going to butter the pavement with them. He was going to carve them like Sunday joints. He was going to take them apart and grind them up for manure.

Martineau, who had been got out of bed and brought to the scene of the crime, watched this remarkable outburst with cool detachment. 'You may be kidding yourself, Dixie,' he mused, 'but you aren't kidding me.'

CHAPTER EIGHT

THAT Saturday morning, after a night of little sleep, Martineau sat down to look at a list of the men who had been released from Farways Prison during the last twelve months. He was appalled to find that he had five hundred and seventy-four names to consider. Of these no fewer than one hundred and ninety could be reckoned as local men, since they lived within ten miles of Granchester Town Hall. In addition, there were many with the description 'no fixed abode' who could be living anywhere. Martineau said "Phew," and settled down to work.

He was agreeably surprised to find that he knew a great many of the local men. In some cases he could remember the crimes for which they had been imprisoned. Some of them had been 'sent down' again, in Granchester and in other towns, and the fact of their safe incarceration could be quickly verified. He began to group the names under districts, to facilitate inquiries.

The names had been listed under different blocks of the big prison, and Martineau remembered that Beadle, Sayers, and Carew had escaped from the north block. He turned to the north list, and was excited to find that George Allott, Owen Blundell, Willis Cooper, Joe Egan, Tommy Straw and Ewart Thompson had all served their sentences in that block. The number of men who had been released from it was one hundred and sixty-two, of whom forty-three were local men and eighteen were of no fixed abode.

Martineau sent for Devery, and together they went through the record cards. Their investigation showed them conclusively that the pursuit of easy money is a dangerous business, with a high mortality rate. Eight of the forty-three local men were already dead, among them being Allott, Cooper, Straw, and Thompson. Of the thirty-five remaining, ten were in prison again, and two had emigrated. On the 'active list' there were the names of twenty-three local men. None of them was a plumber.

Of the eighteen men without homes, ten had been convicted locally. Of these ten, one was dead and four were in prison again.

Martineau made an alphabetical list of the twenty-three and the five, putting beside each name the details of the record card and the prison record. He substituted actual ages for dates of birth, so that a man's age as part of his description would register easily in the mind when the list was read.

When the two lists were completed he started to shorten them, lightly crossing out the following: Czeslaw Chabrowska, convicted of attempted rape; Albert Delarue

Dainton, gross indecency; Josef Nojman, abortion; Rufus Reeder, indecent assault (child).

"That's eliminated the queers for the time being," he said. "Now let's have a look at the snappers-up of unconsidered trifles."

He crossed out the names of six men, most of whom had longish records for small, mean felonies: Thomas Bannister, knife-grinder, larceny of a bicycle; Roger Burnett, general dealer, larceny of washing from a clothes-line; John James Cassidy, tatter, larceny of garden tools; William Oscar Hargreaves, stevedore, dock pilfering; Stanislaus (Stanley) Novak, larceny from a neighbour's shilling-in-the-slot gas meter; Brian Wright, house painter, larceny of a silver pen-and-pencil set.

Thomas Peter Egan qualified for the foregoing group, but Martineau left his name on the list.

"Counting Egan, we're left with eighteen," he said. "Let's see, I think we can cross out these fellows."

He put his pencil through two names, Smith and Connor. Each man had served three years for manslaughter, first offence. Smith was a wealthy company director who had killed a man with his car and failed to stop. Connor had been a prosperous solicitor. An indiscreet love affair with a woman client had led to a quarrel with the woman's husband. A blow struck in anger had caused the husband's death.

There remained sixteen names on the two lists, and Martineau sought to reduce the number still further. Remembering that the Plumber's men would at least have to be youngish and alert, he crossed out the names of four men whom he knew to be too old, too feeble, or too foolish. He also eliminated two men who had records for violence, but not for dishonesty.

"It's crooks we're looking for," he remarked, "and now it's crooks we've got. There are some beauties on this short list. I daresay the Plumber will be using one or two of 'em. They'll give us the lead we want."

There were now only ten names to be considered. Martineau put them in alphabetical order. The first was Owen Blundell, twenty-four years, clerk, of Shirwell; falsification of accounts, twelve months, first conviction. "We'll let him stay on the list because you know his sister," said the inspector with a grin.

Number Two was Martin (Caps) Bowie, thirty-five years, bookmaker's clerk, of Granchester; malicious wounding, three years, ninth conviction. He had slashed his wife's face with a razor. "I fancy him," said Devery. "I tried to get Costello worrying about him." That made Martineau look up thoughtfully. "Oh, you did , did you?" he rejoined. "I wonder if *that* was Ned Higgs's game?"

Next came Irvine Bradley, twenty-nine years, iron-moulder, of Churlham; warehouse breaking, nine months, first conviction with a number of offences taken into consideration. "Never heard of him," Martineau commented. "Nor me," said Devery. "But an ironmoulder could be a likely lad."

Number Four was Thomas Peter Egan, forty-three years, described as a professional wrestler, of Granchester; larceny person, six months, fifth conviction. His had been a crime of proverbial meanness. He had stolen the pitiful takings of a blind beggar.

Next on the list was Thomas Evans, twenty-five years, ship's steward, of Sawford; larceny person (bag snatching), two years, second conviction.

Number Six was Bernard Flint, thirty-seven years, ware-houseman, of Churlham; robbery with violence, seven years, ninth conviction. He had struck down an elderly man with a lead pipe. "A nice guy," Devery remarked.

The next nice guy was Alexander MacFarlane, twenty-eight years, labourer, of Granchester; armed robbery, five years, seventh conviction. He had successfully achieved a single-handed raid on a sub-post office. Fortunately for every-one concerned, including himself, he had not been compelled to shoot anybody.

The next item made both policemen grin: they had been the arresting officers in the case. It was Douglas Savage, forty-two years, cellarman, of the Prodigal Son Inn, Granchester; larceny servant, six months, twelfth conviction. Savage's aged mother, the licensee, made the mistake of sending him to the bank with three days' takings of the inn. The bank was only a hundred yards away, but Doug met friends before he got there. He went to the races with them and, in spite of an almost unrivalled knowledge of equine lineage and past performances, he lost all his money and his mother's as well. In a fury she set the police on him. Later she repented, because she needed his help at the inn. At his trial it was her pleading on his behalf which got him so light a sentence as six months.

"Doug was in Farways with all this lot," said Martineau. "Even if he isn't one of the gang, I'll bet he could give one guess and name the Plumber."

"He'll never talk," said Devery.

Martineau looked wistful. "I wish we could get something on him, and squeeze him."

"You mean frame him?" asked Devery, startled.

"Certainly not! Still, if we could just find something. . . ."

"He wouldn't talk, even then. Not after what happened to the others who might have talked."

"Perhaps you're right, but I'll go for him if I get half a chance. Well, let's see who else we've got here."

Number Nine was Luke Whitehead, thirty-two years, taxi-driver, of Granchester; receiving stolen goods, three years, fifth conviction. He had been associated with a London gang of car thieves. The cars had been stolen and 'reconditioned' in London, and Whitehead had 'flogged' a percentage of them in Granchester.

The last on the list was John Hannah, no fixed abode; forty-three years, fairground worker; armed robbery, three years, eleventh conviction. Like the man MacFarlane, Hannah had raided a post office, but he had been in such haste that he had only taken a small amount of money. "He's worth turning up any time," said Martineau.

"Sure. They all are. But there's one important character missing."

"A big-time fence, you mean? That'll be an out-of-town man, and one of these scoundrels will have a contact with him. Maybe this chap Whitehead, if he still has London connexions. You can sell the hottest stuff in the world there, if you know the ropes. Selling stolen jewellery will be just a doddle."

"We can put a tail on him, after the next job. We've *got* to find the liaison man. Also, we've got to find Beadle and Carew."

"Too true. Could one of those two be the head man of the outfit? Let's look at their records."

Devery had got out the files on Beadle, Sayers, and Carew. He spread them out on a side table, and Martineau gazed at the very clear pictures of three hard-looking men.

"I've gone through these files many a time," said Devery. "They don't seem to have met each other before they were sent to Farways. So we can turn Sayers's face to the wall. He's finished with."

Martineau closed Sayers's file. Sayers had been a Leicester man. Beadle, the safe blower, was a Londoner. Carew, the crack driver, was originally from Bristol. He had operated in London since he had started to steer crooked, but not apparently in the same underworld circles as Beadle. It did indeed look as if the three men had met for the first time in Farways Prison.

Beadle was a slum product, and probably he had been a thief from the day he had found a smaller toddler with a penny in his hand. He had a broad, ugly face and a big jaw. It was not a particularly aggressive face, but neither was it weak. The man was a criminal simply because he had been brought up with criminals and had never heard the Eighth Commandment; nor any other Commandment except the thirteenth. Thou shalt not give information to the bogies.

On the other hand, Carew was a gentleman gone bad, and he looked it. The traditional dissipated handsomeness was there; a certain attractiveness perhaps, and a certain something which might be called breeding. There was recklessness instead of strength, charm instead of honesty, and nonchalance instead of reliability. Carew had been well educated, in the conventional meaning of the term. He was a public school man. Was he, then, the brains behind the Plumber's gang? Was he actually the Plumber?

Martineau knew perfectly well that no amount of ordinary education will make a fool into a wise man, nor a dolt into a clever one. Carew had had his chances in life, Beadle had had none. The brains? If any were there, probably the slum boy had them. Or at least he would have a very effective cunning. With his vast criminal experience, if he were not the Plumber himself he would certainly be the Plumber's lieutenant.

Anyway, that was two of the gang identified. Beadle, Carew, and who else? Owen Blundell and Tom Egan probably. And for the others, Martineau's eye was apt to light on the *violent* criminals on his list: Caps Bowie, Barney Flint, Alex MacFarlane, John Hannah, and Tommy Evans. He felt sure that two or three of those five men would be members of the Plumber's gang. He decided that he would personally make inquiries about them, while Devery, with a wider scope, could nose around after others on the Farways list.

He went to consult Superintendent Clay about this. Clay was pleased with his theory. He looked at the list and talked about making a sudden swoop.

"If we pulled in the lot of them," he said, "we should be able to make at least one of them crack."

Martineau was tempted. If each one of the suspects could be allowed to 'accidentally' see the others in custody, it could lead to the general idea that someone had 'come copper'. At least it would give the impression that the police were in possession of real evidence. One of the suspects might be a softie who would turn Queen's evidence when he thought that the game was up.

"If we did that, we might break up the gang," he said. "But we would scare away Beadle, Carew and the Plumber—whoever he is—with their plunder. They've had the time and money to have the means of escape laid on. They might even have their own boat somewhere. If we pounce on their men, they'll scram."

Clay regretfully agreed. "Yes, I suppose we'd better wait. I'd never raise my head again as a policeman if I let the head murderer get away. But what do you suggest?"

"I'm going to watch some of these fellows very discreetly. So discreetly that I can't possibly raise suspicion. I'll start with the ones I know personally. I'll see where they spend their time, and if they meet anywhere."

"They'll spot you. You're as well-known as the Town Hall clock."

"Ah, but I'm going to do something I've never done before."

"What's that?"

"I'll disguise myself."

Clay stared, and then he laughed. "Sherlock Holmes," he scoffed.

"In all your service in this town have you ever known a policeman to disguise himself?"

"No, never. Not in the way you mean. It's a ridiculous idea."

"That's just why I'd like to do it. Nobody would expect me to do such a thing, you see. Plain glasses with National Health frames; a moustache; hair dyed, or else close-cropped; something in my shoe to give me a limp; pads to puff out my face; sloppy old clothes; the lot."

"No false beard?"

"No. Too noticeable. I could blacken my teeth, though, and spit and chew like any dirty old tatter."

"They'd still recognize you. And they'd rub you out. We'd find your body in the ship canal. I won't allow you to do it. You'll have to find some other way."

"Very good, sir," said Martineau meekly. He picked up his list of names and excused himself.

He left Clay chuckling. "Disguise," the superintendent murmured. "Dearie me, what next?"

On his way through the main C.I.D. office, Martineau stopped at the book cabinet and got out the *Criminal Investigation* of Dr. Hans Gross, late Professor of Criminology of the University of Prague. He carried the book almost surreptitiously into his own office.

CHAPTER NINE

THE following morning, shortly after ten o'clock, the duty clerk in the C.I.D. was busily typing a statement. He became aware that someone was breathing unpleasantly on the back of his neck. He looked round, with a surprise which quickly turned to resentment when he saw the huge, swag-bellied ruffian who was trying to read over his shoulder.

"Get away!" he said sharply, rising quickly to his feet. "That's a confidential document. How did you get in here?"

The man grinned evilly. He seemed to be quite unimpressed by the fact that he was in a police office. "I walked in," he said in a thick voice. "I want to see Superintendent Clay."

"Well you can just inquire at the front office like anybody else. You have no right to be in here."

The man did not cease to grin. "I'm here, ain't I?" he said. "I just want to see this man Clay."

It occurred to the clerk that this cheeky intruder might have to be ejected. He considered him. Strangely brilliant black eyes grinned at him out of a bloated red face, which was made more ugly by a big brown mole on one cheek. Greasy black hair sprouted in neglected tufts from beneath a greasy old cap. Dirty brown teeth showed through a festoon of tobacco-stained moustache. The clerk noticed the tiny gold ear-rings, the dirty muffler, and the deplorable clothes and the shabby boots. And above all he noticed the offensive reek of the man; onions and alcohol. Phew!

"Are you a gypsy?" he asked.

The grin widened. "You know gypsies? Do you speak the language? *Coy minairo coymi?*"

The clerk decided that he would bear the stench of the man no longer, but he doubted if he alone could eject him. He pressed a bell-button to summon the gaoler.

71

"Get out of here!" he said forcefully. "Make your inquiries at the front office."

"Here is where I am, and I want to see this man Clay. And *now* is when I want to see him. *Ring dong bullady macoymi.*"

"You'll see him when you've made a proper appointment. Now, are you going, or do I have to eject you?"

The man was greatly amused. "Inject me? You can't inject *me.*"

'Dead ignorant,' the clerk thought sourly. 'A damned, dirty, stinking, ignorant gypsy. With a knife in his sock, very likely.' He wished that the gaoler would arrive.

"What's your name?" he asked, playing for time.

"*Rim Strim Stramadiddle,* that's my name," said the gypsy, and he laughed idiotically.

The door opened, and two young C.I.D. men came in.

"Oh, get out of here," said the clerk irritably, and he pushed the gypsy.

Mr. Stramadiddle did not cease to smile. He pushed the clerk, who went staggering backward until he fell over his own office stool. The C.I.D. men moved in, one on each side of the intruder. The broad humour of the incident appealed to them, and they were grinning. Nevertheless they held the gypsy fast.

"What's going on here?" one of them asked.

"I just wanted to see Mr. Clay," was the mild reply.

"Get him out of here! Chuck him out!" the clerk bawled from the floor.

"Come on, Petulengro. Out!" said the detective.

The gypsy resisted. He chuckled and gurgled, and made things difficult by putting his foot against an immovable desk. Strangely enough, neither of the detectives succeeded in getting an armlock on him. The gaoler arrived, and he and the clerk joined in the struggle. Some disorder was caused; papers were swept from the desk to the floor, and trodden upon, before they got the gypsy to the door. And there he put his foot against the door frame. The furious clerk kicked his leg, and he was thrust into the corridor. Superintendent Clay emerged from his office.

"What's all this?" he demanded.

The struggle ceased, and the gypsy was temporarily released.

"I just want to see Mr. Clay, that's all," he said.

"I told him to wait out front!" the clerk protested. "He sneaked in there, looking at reports. He wouldn't go out."

"All right, put him out," said Clay, who believed in supporting his men.

"Wait," said the gypsy. "I am a tinker. I can mend pots and pans, and even burst pipes."

"So what? Throw him out."

"All right," said the gypsy, suddenly meek. "If I can't see Mr. Clay, I'll walk out."

"Go on, then. And don't be all day about it."

The gypsy made a small, ironic bow. "*Coy minairo,*" he said, taking his leave.

"What?"

"*Alla bulla ring.*"

"Oh, get out!"

The gypsy went out, humming a tune. He had learned the tune and the words when he was a small boy, from another small boy who had affirmed, probably quite mistakenly, that it was a genuine old gypsy song. He remembered the words quite clearly:

> "*There was a frog lived in a well*
> *With a ring dong bullady macoymi,*
> *There was a frog lived in a well*
> *With a ring dong bullady macoymi.*
> *Coy minairo,*
> *Kilt a cairo,*
> *Coy minairo,*
> *Coymi;*
> *Rim strim stramadiddle alla bulla ring,*
> *Ting-a-ring dong bullady macoymi.*"

Humming his tune, and looking pleased with himself, the raggle-taggle gypsy went in search of the means whereby he could seem to make a living. People gave him plenty of room as he walked through the streets, no doubt because they suspected that he was verminous. He went to the home of one Thomas Bannister, knife-grinder, who had recently been crossed off a police list because he was a criminal of ineffectual calibre. He hoped that Mr. Bannister would have a spare grinding wheel for sale.

Thomas Bannister's wife answered the door. She did not shrink from the gypsy's strange eyes, because she had had a hard life and she had seen all sorts in her time. Her expression was one of militant disapproval, because she assumed that the caller was one of her husband's drunken friends.

" 'E's not in," she said immediately.

"Oh, bullady!" said Stramadiddle, as confident and jaunty as an actor-manager with a booked-up house. "I want to see him on business. I need a grinding wheel."

"Well, I doubt if you'll see Tom for a twelve-month. Two bobbies 'as just been for 'im."

Mr. Stramadiddle was horrified. "Coppers? Dearie me, what's he been doing?"

"Yesterday 'e 'arf-inched a topcoat out of a lady's lobby, the daft article, while she were gone to get 'er scissors for 'im to sharpen. 'E mighta known they'd soon nail 'im for it."

"He won't be needing his wheel, then. Could I hire it?"

"Could you what? An' fade away with it? No fear! You look like a gypsy to me."

"I am a gypsy, but I'm not a poor one. I'll put down a five-pound deposit, and pay ten bob a week for the hire of the wheel."

He produced the money, and the sight of it was too much for the woman. Ungraciously, she agreed to hire out her husband's equipment. The fake gypsy was about to give her five pounds when he remembered that he could not use the wheel on Sunday. He gave her ten shillings, and agreed to call for the wheel and leave the deposit on Monday morning.

After that, Mr. Stramadiddle was made aware, for the first time, of how dreary an English Sunday can be to a rootless stranger. There was nowhere for him to go and nothing for him to do. Fortunately it was a fine morning, and he wandered around in the hope of seeing someone he knew. Once he passed the open door of a church, and a thought made him grin. He could go and rest his feet in there if he liked, but he would certainly not see any friends in there.

Precisely on the hour of noon the pubs opened, and the gypsy began to hunt more hopefully. He knew the places favoured by the men he sought, and he went from bar to bar, not aimlessly but on a pattern which made him almost certain to find one or more of them. He drank mild beer, sparingly. In some places he received hooded, frowning glances which somewhat undermined his satisfaction in his own appearance.

At half-past twelve his old boots clumped along Higgitt's Passage, and he entered the Prodigal Son. He went into the bar lounge, where he was quickly shown the reason for the doubtful glances which he had received. Doug Savage, big, clean, smooth-haired and dapper in a white nylon shirt and grey trousers, looked him over as he approached the bar.

Doug cocked a thumb at him. "Out, Pedro," he said. "Taproom for you."

The gypsy did not protest. He mumbled an apology, and went around to the taproom. It was an open taproom, on the other side of a central bar irregularly oval in shape. Thus Doug could turn away from the lounge bar and serve the people standing at the taproom bar; and thus Mr. Stramadiddle, standing at the taproom bar, could see the people in the bar lounge.

Now that the scruffy stranger had been put in his place, and had humbly accepted it, Doug came and served him civilly enough. "Nice morning," he said as he drew a glass of beer. Just to show that there were no hard feelings.

Stramadiddle had been thinking without bitterness of a social usage which would not allow an apparently honest if dirty pedlar to drink in the company of dressed-up thieves and loose women. He said nothing about that to Doug, but replied in his thick voice that it had been a good summer, and that this fine autumn would make a short winter. Doug nodded, having scarcely heard, and returned to his more affluent customers in the main bar.

The gypsy looked casually around at the taproom

company. There was an old grandad who was cutting twist tobacco while his yet unfilled pipe trembled in toothless jaws. He wore no spectacles, but sat behind his glass of mild ale and peered with eyes almost sightless at a shabby twilight world. There was a young man—whom the gypsy recognized —wearing dirty tennis shoes. He sold newspapers on a corner in Bishopsgate from Monday to Saturday. Now he had a greyhound on a short lead. It was an unresponsive animal but obviously he had a great affection for it. There were two youths who, he thought, had a bad look. They were sniggering over some photographs.

But at the moment the taproom customers were of no interest to him. He looked across at the bar lounge, and saw Caps Bowie talking in a jocose way with a young woman of moderate attractiveness. Both of them appeared to be drinking spirits, an indication that Caps was not short of money. Even so the situation was natural and ordinary enough, and it did not call for the gypsy to do more than have a good look at the girl and memorize her description. He had at least ten minutes to do that, because he knew no one else in the bar lounge and nothing much was happening.

Then another man moved into his view; a man whom he had expected to find only after some difficulty. It was John Hannah, no fixed abode, a violent criminal. He was a man turned forty, with a physique which could be described as 'medium' in every way. His hard face had an ugly lantern jaw and hollow cheeks with the deep vertical furrows of privation.

There may have been privation at some time in Hannah's life, but apparently that time was not the present. It was typical of such a man that he should wear a boldly-patterned tweed suit with a striped tie and a black homberg hat. A proper dandy, Stramadiddle thought mockingly. He was chiefly interested in the fact that the clothes appeared to be brand new. He also noted that the drink which Hannah ordered with such dour nonchalance was a double whisky.

Caps Bowie glanced briefly at Hannah when he ordered the drink, but he did not speak to him. Hannah did not even look at Bowie.

With both men on the list of people in whom he was interested, the gypsy pondered about them, and about their possible connexion with the Plumber. One of the remarkable aspects of the recent run of major robberies had been the absence of 'flash money'. The Plumber had succeeded in imposing at least so much discipline, that none of his irresponsible followers dared to risk drawing attention to himself by abnormal spending or a display of wealth. But the Plumber would not be able to stop his men entirely from enjoying what they considered to be the good things of life, and to a small extent living in a manner to which they were not accustomed. The whisky on the bar in front of Hannah could have been a modified expression of flash money. Stramadiddle remembered that Hannah had once been a trader of sorts. He pretended to a knowledge of antiques, and he was supposed to know a diamond when he saw one. Could he be the man who guided the Plumber's loot into the hands of that big-time fence who lurked in the background?

The gypsy watched for some surreptitious sign of recognition, but saw none. And yet, he thought, those men had served together in the same block at Farways Prison. Surely they would be at least on nodding terms. Their lack of mutual recognition appeared as a suspicious thing. The gypsy made an accurate guess, that the Plumber's men had been ordered not to speak to each other in public places, or to speak as little as possible.

In that respect, it seemed that the Plumber had been a little too careful. He had instigated behaviour which had produced a sort of negative evidence. But that evidence, such as it was, was entirely due to Devery. The behaviour of Bowie and Hannah was only unusual in the eyes of a man who suspected them *and* happened to know that they had been in prison together. It looked as if the Farways list was going to be a bit of bad luck for the Plumber.

There was only a small quantity of beer in the gypsy's glass, but he did not drink it off and order more. He had to be ready to leave at any moment. Hannah might finish his whisky and go. Hannah was his quarry. This was his chance of finding out where the man was living.

77

About this time Mr. Stramadiddle perceived that Caps Bowie had put away two tots of whisky in as many minutes. How long had that been going on, he wondered? The man quite suddenly became noisy and hilarious. So early in the day, less than an hour after opening time, that sort of thing was noticeable. Among others in the bar, Hannah was watching with an impassive face which somehow expressed a measure of disapproval.

Stramadiddle decided that he could order another glass of beer. Neither of his suspects was going to leave the Prodigal Son just yet. Doug Savage amiably refilled his glass, and then immediately he had to go back and refill Bowie's. This, thought the gypsy is where something might break.

He sipped his beer, and Hannah sipped his whisky. Bowie drank his, and had two or three more in the next fifteen minutes. Doug's measures of the spirit became shorter, and the frown of impending refusal appeared on his face. Bowie became quieter. 'Now,' thought the gypsy, 'we start to be sentimental. We might even shed a few tears.'

The only person who seemed to be displeased by Bowie's change of mood was his girl friend. She frowned as he droned confidentially into her ear. Apparently his sentiment was not, so to speak, aimed at her. It was not difficult to guess that he was mourning the wife whose company was denied to him by law.

After some minutes of Bowie's lament, the girl began to look bored. He drank up his whisky once more, and stared sadly at the empty glass. "A happy marriage, all broke up," he said quite loudly. "Her own lawful husband not allowed to pass the time of day with her."

"Oh, you'll get over it," the girl said impatiently.

"I never will," he answered, and suddenly he turned and rushed out of the inn.

Hannah did not appear to see him go, but he finished his own drink, curtly bade 'Good day' to Doug Savage, and went out. The gypsy finished his beer, and followed Hannah.

Because of the day and the hour, there were not many people in the street. The gypsy could see Hannah, and ahead of him, Bowie. He thought that the Northland Hotel was the next calling place, and when he saw Bowie turn the corner into Lacy Street he went along a parallel street and hurried to get ahead. If anything happened at the Northland, it would happen quickly.

He knew that if he entered the hotel by the front door, he would not get past the reception desk in his dirty clothes and boots. He made for the back door of the hotel, and as he went in he calculated that Bowie would now be entering from the front. He passed the 'vaults' where the humbler and rougher customers drank, and made for a part of the hotel where he certainly would not be served. The manager met him in the rear passage and stopped him.

"Where are you going?" was his sharp query. "The vaults are back there."

The stupid Stramadiddle grin appeared. "I've been in the vaults, boss. I'm trying to find my way out of this place."

"In that case you can just turn round and follow your nose. You can't go wrong."

"Can't I go out this way, now I've got so far?" the gypsy asked. He stared around innocently. "By bullady, it's a nice place, is this."

"Your way out is right behind you," said the manager, unrelenting.

The gypsy turned reluctantly, as if he were about to obey. He had no intention of leaving. He was waiting for something to happen.

It happened. A terrible scream rang and rang around the entire floor of the hotel. The manager forgot the gypsy. He went to investigate. The gypsy quietly followed him.

The manager went into the main bar. The gypsy looked in from the doorway. Caps Bowie was at the bar, arguing—or rather protesting—with a waiter. Ella Bowie had retreated to the farthest corner behind the bar. She had stopped screaming, but she still seemed to be in a state of absolute terror. Though her husband was a good six yards away from her, her hands were outstretched as if to hold him off. Her eyes were wide, and her mouth too was stretched wide open, but instead of the scream which seemed about to emerge there was only a panting, sobbing whimper. The half-dozen customers in the bar were watching curiously.

Someone else came to watch from the doorway. It was Hannah. His glance was unguarded and avid as he took in the scene. He had no eyes for the gypsy who stood beside him, and possibly he did not notice him at all.

The manager was a small, neat, forceful man. He strutted across and ranged himself beside the waiter who was obstructing Bowie. "Get out!" he said at once. "You know perfectly well that you're not allowed in here."

"I only came to have a friendly word with my wife," said Caps, alcoholically reasonable but quite determined. He was giving the waiter push for push.

"Get out, or I'll call the police."

"Call the police, then. To hell with the police. They've no right to keep a man away from his lawful wedded wife."

The manager breathed fire: or at least his nostrils distended and his teeth gritted and his eyes flashed. His bluff had been called. For the sake of the hotel's good name he did not want to call the police. His only alternative was to call upon his own staff and throw the man out.

"Get the porter," he commanded. "And get Andre and Ugo from the dining-room."

The waiter hurried away, and the manager remained sternly confronting the intruder. He had time to look round, in a manner intended to be reassuring, at the customers in the bar. Then a cry from Ella startled him. She sank to the floor, apparently having fainted. He looked quickly at Bowie, and turned pale.

Bowie was watching him in a quietly desperate way, and holding his razor in his hand.

"It's gonna be five to one, eh?" he growled. "Five bloody flunkeys to stop a man from having a word with his wife."

He advanced slowly upon the manager, and the manager retreated, with his fascinated gaze upon the razor. Caps held it expertly, gripping the handle in his fingers and letting the blade lie folded back. The holding part of the steel was firm between his thumb and forefinger, and the back of the blade rested on his knuckles. He could strike with that bright blade just as if he were striking a man with his fist: it was the deadliest kind of knuckle-duster ever devised. Caps made experimental circles in the air with it, to the manager's obvious terror.

Then help arrived. It was not Andre or Ugo who came from the dining-room, but Dixie Costello. He shouldered between Hannah and Martineau, and strode into the bar. He went straight up to Caps and slapped him hard across the face.

"Get out of here," he said, angry and contemptuous. "Do you want to get yourself another stretch?"

Caps did not care for that treatment. He scowled, but some fear of Costello or habit of obedience to him made him close his razor. "I only wanted to speak to my wife," he said, surly.

"You're not allowed. Beat it, quick."

"I've a right——"

Costello turned Caps round and bundled him towards the doorway, from which position the gypsy had just moved. He was in the street, standing close to the wall by the hotel entrance, when the boss mobster jostled his henchman through the revolving door.

"Have you gone mad, or what?" Costello demanded. "What are you doing sozzled at this time of day?"

Completely deflated now, Caps stared at his boss without speaking.

Costello went on: "You know Ella screams blue murder every time she sees you, and you can't blame her. The next time you do a trick like that I'll tell the boys to take you apart. I'll have you beautified. Flashing a slicer in the Northland! Do you think I can afford that sort of lark, with things as they are? Just do it again, that's all. Just do it again, and I'll fix you up proper."

With that, Costello went back into the hotel, and Caps wandered disconsolately away down the street. The gypsy moved, to be a little distance from the doorway. He saw Hannah emerge, and stand looking after Caps. He stood still for a full minute, and then he turned and walked purposefully in the opposite direction, towards the gypsy.

Mr. Stramadiddle wondered if Hannah actually had failed
to notice him in the hotel. He reflected that he must not make
the mistake of underestimating the man. He also reflected
that Sunday was a bad day for the business of shadowing a
man; the streets were so empty. He began to walk away
before Hannah reached him, letting the man follow him.
In police jargon, he was 'heading' him instead of 'tailing'
him. As a shadowing device this had sometimes been so
effective that detectives had been able to overhear the
conversation of suspects by walking just in front of them on
a busy street. Today the streets were too sparsely peopled.
Hannah had nobody to look at except the man who walked
in front of him. The gypsy had the feeling of a hostile gaze
boring into his back.

As he walked along he could hear the click of Hannah's
heels on the concrete behind him. For a quarter of a mile he
walked in this way, until he came to the big square which
was also the municipal bus station. There were seats on one
side of the square, and a row of public telephone boxes. He
wondered if Hannah intended to catch a bus. He decided to
let the man get in front of him. He sat down on a seat and
took out his pipe. Hannah walked past him without seeming
to notice him, and went to one of the phone boxes. He
reached to open the box and then stopped with his hand on
the door. It was as if he had suddenly remembered some part
of a lesson in circumspect behaviour. He looked around, and
behind him. The gypsy, not looking at him, felt his cold stare.

He thought: 'Hannah is wondering about me now. And
he is also wondering if a call from a public box can be traced.'

A bus stopped at the kerb in Lacy Street. Hannah walked
across and boarded the bus, and the gypsy had to sit there
and watch him. He had to sit there while the bus drew
away and passed out of his sight by turning along Boyton
Street.

Then he was on his feet. By great good fortune there was
a taxi coming along. He flagged the taxi. The driver looked
at him, and pursed his lips as if he were making a rude noise,
and went on his way. The gypsy cursed, and vowed that he
would 'book' the taxi driver. Then he remembered his own

appearance. He could not really blame the taxi driver for refusing to pick him up.

Hannah the man of no fixed abode had been found and lost. But the gypsy had the consolation of being tolerably certain that he now knew the names of six members of the Plumber's gang.

Beadle, Carew, Egan, Blundell, Bowie, Hannah.

And Hannah was about to report Bowie's bad conduct to the Plumber. Bowie might shortly become the subject of a harsher discipline than Dixie Costello's.

CHAPTER TEN

AT midday there were not many customers in the establishment known as Jimmy Ganders. A dozen people in that long room made it seem almost empty. The curious and the lonely and the men in search of promiscuous girls were not there in the daytime. The customers were nearly all regulars, and they were all people who did not lead normal workaday lives.

There were two prostitutes taking their first look at the day. They were off duty; smartly dressed and made up, but not for the purpose of attracting men. When they pursued their trade they went elsewhere and at night, and only in the daytime if they were short of money. These two were not short of money. They talked grandly of going to the Royal Lancaster Hotel for lunch. It was even money that they would not get past the porter at the Royal Lancaster.

The prostitutes were two-thirds of the way along the bar, exchanging the gossip of the day with one of the two barmen. All the other customers were between them and the dais at the far end of the room, clustered in one-third of the room as if they derived comfort from herding together.

At the far end of the bar, leaning sideways upon it so that he could see the entire room, was the gypsy knife-grinder who had been around the centre of the town for the last few days. He had smartened himself up a little since Sunday, and as long as he behaved himself he was tolerated in Jimmy Ganders. He behaved himself. He was civil when spoken to, and he did not try to butt into the conversations of others.

At the bar between the prostitutes and the gypsy was Owen Blundell, in company with a girl who went by the name of Sally Morgan. She was blonde and pretty, and so young that she looked as if she were on the plump, ripe threshold of womanhood. Actually she had crossed the threshold long before the age of consent, and now she lived with Alex MacFarlane. She was telling Blundell that yesterday Alex had gone to Glasgow to see his mother. He would be returning to Granchester sometime today.

"Confound it!" said Blundell, who was of a type to talk like that. "I wish I'd known he was away. I'd have come up to see you."

"Oh, you would, would you?" she retorted, pleased but ostensibly disapproving.

There was a glint in young Blundell's eye. "You're a nice girl, Sally. I've always had a fancy for you."

"Only a fancy?"

"Well, you know. . . ."

"You wouldn't like me to tell Alex, would you?"

"You wouldn't do that."

"Oh, I might."

"Well, if you're going to be like that, I'm getting out of here."

"No. Don't go yet, Owen. I'm only kidding."

And so on. The gypsy listened.

Sitting at a table with two other men, one of whom was a bookmaker's runner, was John Hannah. He was looking at the racing page of a newspaper, and commenting on the day's runners and riders. At another table, sitting alone but also studying horses and jockeys, was Caps Bowie. He was quite sober. He had a pint glass of strong beer on the table in front of him.

It was a fortuitous gathering of suspects, but not strange because Jimmy Ganders was one of their places. Everyone except the gypsy was moderately content. The gypsy liked a pint of beer himself, but he was weary of the everlasting pub crawl of the criminal classes. Pubs, pubs, clubs and pubs, and dingy ones at that. To himself he repeated the well-known complaint of the barmaid at closing time: 'Ain't you got no homes?'

Into this place, and this peaceful if not idyllic scene, walked Detective Sergeant Devery. He stood just inside the door, eyeing the company. There was a general hiatus in conversation which even the racing students sensed, and they looked up from their papers.

Devery seemed to count heads. He saw the gypsy and knew who he was. He was the only man in Granchester, besides the gypsy, who did know. He decided that he had better not stay. He pondered for a moment. Would he have a quick drink and then go away, or would he go immediately? It would be better perhaps to give the impression that he was looking for one certain person, who was not present in Jimmy Ganders. He decided on that. Having looked at everyone, he turned and walked out.

Such was the condition of the consciences of those people that it was at least half a minute—until everyone was sure that he had gone—before the tension broke. It was the women who were heard first, with comments and questions. Having less to fear than the men, but disliking the police from childhood, they gave utterance to their facile indignation. The burthen of their chatter was: "What does he want in here? Spoiling everybody's fun!"

"He has a warrant for somebody, happen," the barman informed the two prostitutes.

"I don't know, and I don't care," Owen Blundell told the girl Sally.

But the abrupt intrusion, followed by the bad moment when he had wondered if the hard, probing glance could be seeking him personally, had made him change colour. The girl did not fail to notice.

"You've gone white," she said, with some derision.

Blundell was annoyed. The girl's observation had pricked his vanity. He could not help but look around to see who had heard her. He saw the gypsy watching him. The gipsy was a very big man, but he was obviously a person of no account.

"What the hell are you staring at?" Blundell demanded.

The gypsy grinned stupidly, shrugged, and looked away. This suggestion of withdrawal from argument encouraged Blundell.

"Dirty wog," he said loudly. He glared fiercely.

The gypsy seemed not to have heard him. A barman said: "Simmer down, kid. He never did you any harm."

There was an interruption, by a newcomer. He had entered quietly, and during the brief disturbance he had made his way unnoticed along the bar. He was a small, dark young man with shallow wolfish eyes.

"What goes on?" he asked, in the accent of Clydeside.

"That bloke," said Blundell, nodding towards the gypsy. "Who is he, anyway?"

The newcomer favoured the gypsy with a glance. "Yeh, I've wondered. He seems to be around an awfu' lot."

But the Scotsman was prepared to let the gypsy wait for his attention. He looked at the two glasses on the bar, and at the girl Sally. His girl.

"I just met him, Alex," she said. "We were just talking. I bought my own drink."

There was no sign of anger in Alex MacFarlane's face, but with a sort of deliberate quickness he slapped the girl hard across the mouth with the back of his hand. She fell back a pace. "Pig!" she said, and she reached for an empty beer bottle which was standing on the bar.

The barman who had spoken to Blundell caught her wrist and deftly removed the bottle. "Outside, if you want to fight," he said firmly.

MacFarlane had been quite unmoved by the girl's gesture. "You know I don't talk to this half-inch tango tiger," he said with unfeeling reasonableness, "but the minute my back is turned you're clinking glasses with him. Did you have him in bed with you last night?"

"I did not!" the girl flared. "Don't you dare say such a thing, Alex MacFarlane!"

The answer seemed to satisfy MacFarlane. He turned to Blundell, a man a head taller than himself. "Away, fellow," he said.

That was too much for Blundell's pride. "I don't take orders from you," he said sullenly.

"You *got* your orders," said MacFarlane, forcefully and with meaning. "Get away!"

Blundell made a token withdrawal: he moved a little way along the bar. After that the little Scot ignored him, and turned and went to the gypsy. He looked up at the gypsy, a man big enough to eat him for breakfast.

"Who are you, anyway?" he demanded.

The gypsy smiled faintly, and did not reply.

MacFarlane's glance narrowed. He moved closer, looking up. "You got funny eyes," he said, scrutinizing the big man's face with detached interest. Then he moved, with the lightning quickness of a bantam-weight fighter. His hand shot out, and then the gypsy's moustache lay in his upturned palm.

"A dirty spy," he said, and that was all he had time to say. The bogus gypsy had shifted his weight from the elbow which rested on the bar. The right fist chopped down, and little MacFarlane tottered backward and fell, having been hit by the hardest hitter among the thousand hard hitters of the Granchester police.

Hannah and Bowie were on their feet. Blundell had slipped his hand inside his coat. Then Hannah sat down again, and Bowie did the same. Blundell observed Hannah's move, and met his gaze. The older man shook his head very slightly, and Blundell hastily removed his hand from his coat. Everyone else in the room had remained quite still. Everyone, that is, except the gypsy.

From his corner the gypsy had seen everything, and without taking his eyes from the people around him he had reached over the bar to a shelf beneath it, from which he had seen the barmen take one-pint bottles of beer. He picked up a bottle of beer by the neck, and held it so. Then, because there did not seem to be any great hurry, he took a two-shilling piece from his pocket and laid it on the bar, to pay for the bottle. Then, bottle in hand, he started to walk to the door.

No one obstructed him. He stepped around the prostrate MacFarlane and walked past the tables, and past Blundell.

He did not turn his head, but he was alert, concentrating on the faculty of hearing. But no one moved, and soon there was no one between him and the door except Ned Higgs, who had just entered.

Higgs stood by the door, an interested spectator. As the gypsy approached he stepped smartly aside. He looked hard at the gypsy, but he did not speak.

The gypsy passed him, then turned at the door and presented him with the bottle of beer. "Have a drink," the gypsy said, then he put his shoulder to the swing door and was gone.

Higgs walked down the room and put the bottle on the bar. "Pour that into a schooner for me," he said to one of the barmen.

"I wonder what that fellow's game was," said the barman, pleasantly excited. "Going about in a false moustache."

"He's a copper," said Higgs, not troubling to lower his voice.

There was silence in the bar. The only movement was made by Sally Morgan, who was nursing MacFarlane's head and dabbing his forehead with a handkerchief soaked in gin.

"Ah, but what sort of a copper?" the barman persisted. "One of these private eyes?"

Higgs looked disgusted. "Private eyes!" he said. "Godelpus, are you all blind? It was Martineau, done up like a dog's dinner."

The silence in the room was intensified. People there were wondering; wondering what the police knew of their recent activities. Those who did not know Martineau had heard of him. Hannah, Blundell, and Bowie looked at each other. In their eyes there was doubt, distrust, and consternation.

Higgs did not miss any of Bowie's reaction. 'All right, Caps boy,' he said to himself. 'We've got you taped. When I tell Dixie, your name's McCoy.'

*　*　*　*　*

From Jimmy Ganders Devery went to the Empress Billiard Hall, and from there to the Bolero Club, and from there to the Slip In Café. He looked in Chu's Chinese Restaurant and the Sahara Coffee Bar. In none of those places did he see anything of interest to him. When he was passing the Northland Hotel he thought he would call in there.

In Ella's bar there were eight or nine customers. She was not busy. She smiled when she saw Devery, and he was pleasantly surprised. He was so pleasantly surprised that when he ordered his glass of beer he asked her if she would have a drink. She accepted. Gin, as usual.

"Well, well," he said genially. "Things are looking up. I thought you didn't like me."

"What, a good-looking lad like you?" she replied. "Any girl would go for you."

"Now you're taking the mickey."

"Oh, no, I'm not," she said, but there was laughter in her eyes.

"All right then. What about that night off I keep harping about?"

"Sure. Tomorrow night. You can take me out."

That made him pause. "Well, I'll be damned. That this chance should come at such a time! You know how busy we are. I won't be able to get off till ten o'clock at least."

"Well, you're a bright article. Asking for a date you can't keep."

He smiled ruefully. "The bad luck is mine. But keep the date open for next week, for Pete's sake. I'll probably be free then."

"What time will you be off duty tonight?"

"Oh, ten o'clock, if all's quiet."

"Come in for a drink, then you can walk me home when I finish work."

"I'll be here," said Devery with alacrity. "Have another drink, Ella."

* * * * *

While Devery lingered with Ella in the Northland, three of his suspects were sitting in the Central Ward Working

Men's Club. They had gone there separately, by different routes, and they had chosen the place for two reasons. It was a genuine club which the police could not enter without a warrant, and MacFarlane's girl could not follow them there. They sat in a corner of the deserted billiard room and talked in subdued voices. They were disobeying orders, but this was a crisis.

MacFarlane was speaking of Martineau, the man who was on all their minds. "He can't know anything," the little Scot argued. "He didn't see nothing important. None of us were buttying up together. I had a few words with Owen here, but they weren't the sort to make anybody think we were pals, were they?"

"We could have give ourselves away," said Bowie gloomily. "After he banjoed you, Owen reckoned to go for his gun. He shouldn't a-been carrying a gun at all."

"He never saw me," Blundell protested. "I never took my eyes off him. He was watching you and John."

"Well, we only stood up and sat down again. Anybody might do that."

"Yeh, sure," said MacFarlane confidently. "It was a good thing you kept your heads and let him go. I was the mug. I should never have let him hit me."

"You did well to spot him," Bowie conceded. "Whoever would have expected a top copper like Martineau to go around in disguise?"

"Well, he'd sort of sprung from nowhere, and he'd been around too much for my liking. But I guess I was as surprised as anybody when his moustache came off. Anyway, he was spotted before he got to know anything. Unless we've got a grasshopper amongst us."

They looked at each other.

"Nobody's come copper," said Blundell, the least formidable but the most intelligent of the three. "If somebody had blabbed, there'd be no need for Martineau to go about looking like somebody who's just been ten years in a dungeon."

Reassured, the others nodded. "I wish John 'ud be quick." said Bowie.

Blundell went to get some beer. They were on their second round of drinks when Hannah arrived, and joined them.

"What does he say?" Bowie asked anxiously.

Hannah's wintry grin appeared. "He says we ought to have our heads looked at for all being in the same place at once. But apart from that we didn't do so bad. He said you did very well, Mac."

MacFarlane looked pleased. "What else?" he asked.

"I had to tell him the whole thing from start to finish, every little bit of it, who was there and everything. He said it could have been worse. He also said it was time we wrapped up."

There was a murmur of approval.

"There's just one more job tomorrow night. He didn't say where it was, but we can all retire on it. We'll touch a quarter of a million in cold cash. Every man will receive his detailed instructions in the usual way, by word of mouth from Owen or Gracie, or from the boss himself."

"Gracie," said MacFarlane doubtfully.

"Oh, she's all right," said Blundell. "It was jealousy. She wouldn't have blabbed anything important, anyway."

"I don't trust any woman," said the Scot.

"Neither do I, and I don't have one hanging around," said Hannah, pointedly to MacFarlane. "But if the boss says Gracie is all right, that's all there is to it. He's never been wrong yet. By the way, Owen, tomorrow night you'll be on the job as well. All hands on deck."

Blundell's face reflected dismay, then he set his lips and nodded hardily.

"A quarter of a million nicker," said Caps Bowie, lost in a dream of wealth. "Where will he find us that much money?"

Of the four, only one lived in anything like a home, where thrift was a virtue and shopping a matter for careful thought. Blundell was the only one who could even make a guess.

"The Eco," he said.

The others stared at him.

*　　*　　*　　*　　*

91

"Where have you been?" Superintendent Clay demanded.

"Working under cover," Martineau replied. "I rung in, didn't I?"

"But nobody has seen you anywhere. A man like you can't move about unseen in Granchester."

"Well, I did move about."

Clay's eyes narrowed suspiciously. "Your hair is a funny colour," he said. "Have you been trying to disguise yourself, against my orders?"

Martineau nodded. "It was all for the cause. Default me if you like. I'll take the Chief's punishment."

"Hmmm. What happened?"

"I was spotted. Today."

"I told you so."

"You didn't spot me, anyway."

"Me? I never saw you."

"Yes you did. You saw me in the corridor outside this office."

"In a disguise? I did not!"

"You did, sir. Last Sunday morning."

"Well, I don't recollect."

"You had me thrown out of the building."

Clay stared. "That was you? I don't believe it."

"It was I," said Martineau.

"But that fellow had eyes like black buttons. You can't alter the colour of your eyes, except with contact lenses. And you can't get those at five minutes' notice."

"You're forgetting your Hans Gross, sir."

Clay became thoughtful. "I remember," he said after a pause. "*Practices of Criminals*. They used atropine to dilate the pupils of blue or grey eyes until none of the iris was visible, so that they appeared to have dark eyes. Atropine! I hope you didn't do anything so damn silly."

"No. I went to see Dr. Mackenzie, and took him into my confidence to a small extent. He wouldn't give me atropine. He said that it could bring on a disease of the eyes called glaucoma. He used some other stuff which was quite safe."

"And how did you get your eyes back to normal?"

"Eserine. That's the stuff for contracting the pupil."

"And are you all right now?"

"Yes, I think so. I m right glad to get back to normal."

"I should think so. You had a belly bigger than mine. What did you use?"

"Pillows, firmed up by a pair of the biggest corsets you ever saw in your life. It was a bit warm."

"It serves you right. What was that thing on your face?"

"The mole? That was pure Hans Gross. A mixture of grated leather and glue. It looked very natural, didn't it?"

Martineau went on to explain that his blond hair, grey at the temples, had happened to need cutting. He had simply dyed it black, greased it, and left it uncombed. He had darkened and reddened his face with strong coffee and permanganate of potash. His attempts to disguise his voice had been assisted by mouth pads and a great piece of chewing gum. His disreputable clothes, like the outsize corsets, had been procured by his wife. His boots had been an old pair which had been standing on a shelf in his garden shed for several years.

"A bit amateurish," he said. "But the only weakness in the entire get-up was the false moustache. And it was that which let me down. Julia stuck it on for me as well as she could, though."

Clay nodded. Mrs. Martineau was completely trustworthy about any matter which concerned her husband's career.

"I'll bet she laughed when she saw the finished product," he remarked.

"She didn't," said Martineau seriously. "She looked a bit scared. It was the eyes, I think."

"I'm not surprised. I still think you were barmy to do it. And what have you found out?"

"Not much. I have no evidence at all. But I've seen enough to make me certain that we're on the right track. It's all sort of psychological. Little things. Little bits of behaviour."

"Psychological my eye! I want some evidence."

"You wait till I've compared notes with Devery. I think we'll be able to move in on those clients."

"You do?"

"Sure. We'll be Johnny-on-the-spot when they got to do their next job."

*　　*　　*　　*　　*

"I haven't got much, sir," said Devery. "I've eliminated some characters from the secondary list. Also, I went to Winter's and hired the littlest camera you ever saw, and I've got a few pictures of suspects in conversation with others. If there are associates who aren't on our list, we may have got pictures of them."

Martineau shook his head. "I'm not belittling your efforts," he said, "but unless my observations are entirely based on a misapprehension, it's a certainty that the Plumber's men have been ordered to ignore each other in public."

"That lets this fellow out, then," said Devery, pushing forward a photograph.

The picture showed two men standing in the street. One was passing something to the other, quite openly. The giver was a tall, powerfully built, handsome man in his late thirties. The receiver was about the same age, a small man with the flat profile of a Slav.

"What is it?" Martineau asked.

"A box of matches. The little man stopped the big fellow and said something to him. I thought he asked for a light, because Big Fellow handed him the box of matches and waited while he took one out, lit a cigarette, and handed the box back. That's all. The little man just nodded his thanks, and they went their ways."

"What made you take a picture?"

"The big boy is Robert Connor. The little Pole is Stanley Novak. You crossed both of them off your Farways list. They were both in the North block, at the same time."

"And they seemed to act as if they were strangers to each other?"

"I'd say so. Connor never spoke at all. He didn't even pass the time of day. Just handed over the matches and took them back."

"And yet those two men *must* know each other. Enough

to say 'How are you doing?' at any rate. It's the Plumber's technique, all right. There could have been a message in the matchbox. When did you take the picture?"

"Today. It's the last one I took."

"So, if this means anything, there's going to be another job quite soon. Have you anything else on those two?"

"On Connor, I have. I was in Shirwell Tuesday evening, trying to get a line on that ex-insurance man who's on my list. I saw the Blundell girl getting on a bus. I got the number of the bus, and went into a phone box and got Headquarters to send an area patrol car to pick me up. When the A. P. car caught up with the bus I contacted H.Q. again, and asked for a plain car to meet me in Somerset Square. We followed the bus into town, and the girl got off at the terminus in Somerset Square. I picked up the plain car and followed her. She went to the house where Robert Connor has a flat. She didn't come out till nearly midnight."

"H'm. There seems to be some sort of connexion, but it's dodgy. At one time that girl was supposed to be about to tell *you* something over the phone."

"Yes, that puzzles me. But I don't know just what she was going to tell me, do I? It might have been another of the Plumber's false alarms. Besides, it's nearly a fortnight ago. There can be a change of heart in a fortnight."

Martineau was doubtful. He picked up the photograph again. "I recognize Connor now," he said. "He's changed a bit."

"Disgrace and imprisonment. Pride in the gutter."

"Yes. He was a bit of a bighead when he was doing well as a lawyer. Trouble of that sort would hit him hard."

They talked about Robert Connor. As a prosperous solicitor, unmarried, he had been tempted into a love affair with one of his clients, a married woman with money and property. The woman's husband had become suspicious, and he had caught the two together. In the subsequent quarrel, Connor knocked the man down. It was the only blow struck, and Connor was much the bigger man and he was the aggressor. The man happened to have a brittle skull, and he died. The woman had had some sort of affection for her husband in spite of her infidelity, and she turned against Connor. Her evidence, and the circumstances, got him three years imprisonment. What he would regard as her betrayal of him must have increased Connor's bitterness against the world.

"Before he went to prison he did a certain amount of police-court work," Devery pointed out. "He defended quite a number of crooks with success. He had a good name amongst the riff-raff."

"I see what you mean," said Martineau. "What was his job in Farways?"

Devery smiled. "They didn't make a plumber of him. As a man of education, he was put in the prison library."

"In the library! That's an ideal position for directing a mob. He could receive and transmit messages without raising the slightest suspicion. But would a man of his upbringing have any use for a clown like Bowie or a treacherous weakling like Blundell?"

"Why not, so long as he is one of the bosses. He's not a lawyer now, you know. He's an outcast, and nobody will be more aware of it than himself."

"You're hinting that if he's in the job at all, he *is* the Plumber."

"Well, he has the brains to organize, and enough knowledge of police and criminals to avoid the usual errors, and enough ascendancy over men like Bowie to make *them* avoid errors."

"And why does he call himself the Plumber?"

"Because he's nothing like a plumber. If he called himself the Librarian or the Lawyer it would be a clue, wouldn't it?"

Martineau sighed. "I'll go along with you, but we haven't the slightest shred of evidence. We don't even know if the wench who started all this was the same wench who tried to phone you. There could have been a dozen girls with black eyes walking about Granchester that day."

"I'll chance a bet on it," said Devery stubbornly. "She'd been hammered. She was in a panic. She knew me when she saw me. She ran away from me. She has a gaolbird brother and a gaolbird lover. Yes, I'll chance it."

96

"All right, all right. We'll continue to look at it that way. You've been the boy with the bright ideas all along. If everything works out fine, I guess you'll get a cartload of commendations. Now buzz off."

Devery went. Martineau sat in thought. Idly he wrote down names: Beadle, Carew, Blundell, Bowie, Egan, Hannah, MacFarlane, Connor, Novak.

CHAPTER ELEVEN

IF any extraordinary deployment of police manpower was made that night, it did not include Devery. At first he was uneasy about this. If there was to be a job tonight, he wanted to be in action. He went around. He saw Alex MacFarlane in the Las Vegas Club with his girl, and MacFarlane was drinking. Outside the club, standing close together in a shop doorway like lovers, were the newest policewoman on the force and a young C.I.D. man from an outer division. They gave him no sign of recognition as he passed the doorway, but he murmured, "Don't overdo it," and heard a tiny snicker of laughter from the girl.

Devery walked on. He looked along the first side street and saw a car. He went that way, and recognized the car as one which he had often driven. There were two men in the car. So with one thing and another it appeared that Mr. MacFarlane was being looked after.

If MacFarlane was under surveillance, then so would be Hannah, Bowie and the rest. Devery ceased to bother his head about them. He returned to Headquarters, and learned that Martineau was in session with Clay and the Chief. Martineau, it seemed, was 'going along' as he had promised. There might be action tonight, but tomorrow night was more likely. Tomorrow night. Friday.

Devery took the opportunity to do some paper work and bring his official diary up to date. At half-past nine he was, as he said to himself, abreast of the times. He went round to the front office and learned that Martineau was still in session with the bosses. Big plans, apparently. Devery had been working since nine o'clock that morning so he could sign off with an easy conscience. He signed off, and thankfully left the building.

He went to the Northland Hotel. Ella was very busy, but she gave him a special smile as he made his way to the end of the bar. Her greeting was roguish when she came to serve him, and she agreed to have a drink with him. She had time to take only a small sip of her drink before she had to go off and serve someone else.

He leaned on the bar and watched her with pleasure. The shape of her delighted him, and there was something specially attractive about the way she moved. She was handsome, and he reflected that her scar did not really spoil her; it merely made her different from other women. He admitted to himself that he wanted her rather badly. He had no idea how long the affair would last—if it was to be an affair—and he did not dwell upon the matter. He knew that he was acting foolishly from a career point of view: she was a married woman, and her husband was a criminal. He did not dwell upon that, either. He dwelt upon Ella, and her strong shapely legs, and her movements, and her smile. She pretended to have a fellow somewhere. Somehow he did not think there was a fellow. Anyway, that was her business.

Ella managed to finish her drink during hurried visits to Devery's end of the bar, and she accepted another one. She had not finished that at closing time, and she had to take time off to drink it when she had finished serving the last rush of customers.

"You made it, then," she said, as she took her place across the bar from him. "I wondered if you'd been too busy."

"I made it," he said solemnly. "I got special leave."

"Pooh," she said.

"I've worked a thirteen-hour day. I could do with a drink or two. How about us taking a bottle of something along to your place?"

"What makes you think you'll be staying?" she asked coolly.

"If we have something to drink I'll have to stay to drink it, won't I?"

"I don't know. There's no need to take anything, anyway. I have as much in as you'll want."

"And as much as *you'll* want?"

She smiled. "Yes."

When the glasses had been gathered, and washed, and polished, Ella slipped on a loose coat and announced that she was ready to go home. She took his arm confidingly as they walked along Lacy Street. Devery hoped that they would not meet any senior police officers—'It's a hell of a profession, is mine,' he thought—but he did not greatly care if they did. Such can be the effect of a few drinks and a desirable woman upon an ambitious young man.

The walk was less than half a mile. Ella was, and always had been, a middle-of-towner. She lived in one of the many streets of late Victorian houses which had been turned into furnished rooms and small flats. She had a two-room flat, and the three flights of stairs leading up to it had a very worn carpet. But the flat itself was bright enough; furnished cheaply, but comfortably and in moderately good taste.

She invited him to enter, and then she closed the door. She stood, with her hands in the pockets of her loose coat, and smiled at him. "Would you like me to make you a bit of supper?" she asked.

To Devery she was irresistible. "No," he said. He reached for her and pulled her to him. He held her around the waist. She leaned back in his arms and looked at him archly.

"My goodness," she said. "He doesn't even give a girl time to take her coat off."

* * * * *

Martin Caps Bowie sat before the gas fire in his dingy furnished room and thought about his future, and about his wife. His future, which was hopeful, and his wife, who had become an obsession and a voluptuous dream, were inextricably tangled in his mind. He wanted her to come back to him, and yet he was not allowed to speak to her. It seemed to him that the best thing he could do would be to write a letter. Could she have him up in front of a magistrate for that? Would they say that he was pestering her by post? No, he decided. Not for just one letter.

Now, he had something to offer Ella. Money was a lure which few women could resist. He had plenty, and after tomorrow night he would have lots more. He would be rich. And tomorrow's job would be the last. He was relieved about that. The business was getting too risky. The police were getting too near for comfort. And besides, there was Dixie Costello. Dixie was very fly. If the thing went on, he would get the griff sooner or later. And he permitted no sidelines which were not known to him. He would regard membership of another gang, behind his back, as high treason. If Dixie found out, it would be curtains for Caps Bowie.

For several years Caps had nursed a dream about a certain racing system. All that he needed to operate the system had been capital. Now, he had the capital. With that behind him, he knew that he could not go wrong. He would go to race meetings, and he would become a rich and respected figure. And Ella would go with him. She used to like to go to the races. When she knew how much money he had, she would come back to him, and they would be happy again.

He began to consider the terms of his letter to Ella. He would tell her that he loved her and would not hurt a hair of her head, and that he wanted her back. He would throw away his razor if she would return to him. He would never hurt her again; never lay a finger on her; he had had his lesson. He would say that he had been doing well on the horses, that he had had a phenomenal season, that he had thousands of pounds spread out in a dozen bank accounts, and that he was saving the money for her. He would promise her a fur coat and a diamond ring, and he would buy a nice little house for her.

He had no doubt that he would get her back. The money would get her back. After tomorrow night, he would start a new life with Ella.

Without getting up from his chair he reached for the

cheap writing-pad which he had placed in readiness on the mantelpiece. He calculated that if he posted the letter before he went to bed, it would be collected early and Ella would receive it by the midday delivery. He took a stub of pencil from his pocket, and he began to write.

*　　*　　*　　*　　*

Alex MacFarlane sat in the only armchair in the furnished room which he occupied with Sally Morgan. Sally sat on a stool on the opposite side of the small bedroom fireplace. They were having the cup of tea upon which she always insisted before bed. She was perched on the stool gracelessly but comfortably, with her knees apart and her skirt carelessly rucked, so that she showed her excellent legs up to the thigh.

The night's drinking had left her surly. She was remembering noontime's unavenged slap on the face. And that was only one of a tally of grievances and suspicions.

"You never said how your mother was," she observed sulkily.

"Oh, she's all right," he replied. He had not seen his mother for years; not since he had been drummed out of his father's old regiment, the Cameron Highlanders. But he used his mother's name as an excuse for going to Glasgow. He banked his money in Glasgow, because that was where he intended to flee if ever flight became necessary. Seeking him in his home town, the police would contact his mother. She would tell the truth, that she had seen nothing of him. Then the police would conclude that he was not in Glasgow at all. They would not find him there, at any rate. He knew where he could hide until the police were tired of looking for him.

"You've got a woman in Glasgow," was Sally's sudden accusation.

"Sure," he said. "The old woman who bore me."

"Nobody would go all that way just to see his mother," she persisted. "You've got a woman there. That's why you never take me with you."

"There aren't two spare beds. We couldn't sleep together in my mother's house."

"We could stop at a hotel."

"All right," he said. "The next time I go, I'll take you."

She was silent for a while, then she said: "When are you going out again?"

"What the hell are you talking about?" he demanded. He never told her when he was going to join the gang on a job. He just eluded her, and went. And when he returned, he never allowed her to question him.

"I'm not daft," she said. "I know, you know."

Alex had been drinking the last of his tea, looking into the cup as he drank. He turned his head and looked at her.

"And what is it you know?" he demanded with heavy sarcasm.

"Every time you've been out at night there's been one of those big robberies in the paper. You're one of that gang."

Then she quailed. His expression frightened her.

"Do you know what you're saying?" he asked softly. "Do you know what happens to folks who think they know something about that lot? They get rubbed out. Croaked; finished; murdered. They'd cut your throat so your head fell off if they knew what you'd just said."

"I didn't say nothing," she whimpered. "I wouldn't tell."

"You accused me. You put me in with that mob. Och, woman, you must be mad!"

But he was the one with something like madness in his eyes. She saw murder there, and she was terrified.

"No, I didn't," she wailed. "I didn't accuse you. I won't say nothing again. Honest I won't."

He slapped her. She took the blow, and sat with the eyes of a frightened doe so that he could slap her again if he liked. She knew the danger. She had to show him that she was his woman, who would never betray him.

His fury and suspicion were softened by contempt. She was only a woman. "Go to bed," he snapped.

She stood up and kicked off her shoes, and then without moving from where she stood she began to undress. He picked up a newspaper and began to read the sports page.

She took off all her clothes, and then she felt better. Alex was looking at tomorrow's horses. The danger had passed. The thing had blown over.

She picked up a hair brush, then returned to her stool and began to brush her mass of blonde hair.

"Are you coming to bed, Alex?" she asked.

He looked at her. Her youthful figure was perfect. Her ankles were dirty.

"I'll come in a minute," he said. Take her to Glasgow? In a pig's eye he would. She'd had it. Her name was Walker.

But he had to fix her up so that she would not run squealing to the cops after he had kicked her out. He had to think of some way to stop her mouth for good. He dared not kill her, because he had quarrelled with her so often and so publicly that he would be immediately suspected. If he gave himself an unbreakable alibi while someone else killed her, there would still be a lot of police questions. He did not want that. He did not want the limelight.

He thought about what he could do with her. She observed the fixity of his glance, and she knew that he was not reading. His whole face was intense with the effort of thought. She shivered. The thing had not blown over after all. He was brooding about it. He might get real mad and start laying his feet into her. She went and got into bed, and sat there brushing her hair.

He put down the paper and sat staring at the dead cinders in the fireplace. Sally put away her hairbrush and settled her head on the pillow. But she did not dare to close her eyes. She was too much afraid of the man who sat there in absolute stillness, thinking.

Presently MacFarlane stood up and started to undress. With half-closed eyes she watched him. Fear made her imagination run wild, and she was prepared for anything. She was relieved when he dropped his tie into a drawer, because he had once showed her how he could whip off his tie and neatly garrotte a person with it. But when he got into bed beside her she did not withdraw from him. She had courage of a sort.

"He said: "Oh hell, I forgot the light. Turn it out, will you Sally?"

She did not want the light out. "I'll turn it out in a minute," she said. "When I've got warm."

He grunted and snuggled down. She lay staring at the ceiling, counting. He had been indulging in the Scots habit of drinking chasers. He had had at least ten glasses of whisky and quite a lot of beer. He would sleep heavily, she thought.

He seemed to go to sleep straight away. As she lay listening to his breathing she had a struggle to keep her own eyes open. She began to wish that she had not had so much to drink. It could make her clumsy, and spoil everything.

Soon he was snoring. She waited. The snores were real enough, she thought. Surely a man could not pretend to snore for any length of time.

When she was sure that he slumbered, she slipped out of bed. She made sure of his money first, a small wad which he had left in his trousers pocket. She made a quick estimate of the amount, about twenty-five pounds. She peeled off one note and replaced it in his pocket with a trembling hand. The strain was terrible: she thought that he would surely kill her if he caught her robbing him. But when she began to dress she felt better. She slipped the wad of notes into the top of her stocking.

Nearly dressed, she began to feel gleeful and confident. She knew where she could get a bed even at this late hour, and tomorrow she would leave town. She knew a girl who was reported to be doing well in London. If Bertha Wrigley could make a living in London, with her looks, what could Sally Morgan do? It would be easy. The thought of it was exciting. To hell with Alex MacFarlane.

A choking snort interrupted his snore, and her heart seemed to stop. She stood quite still, staring at him. His eyes opened and he looked at her, but he did not seem to see her. He turned over, and began to breathe heavily again.

She picked up her handbag and tiptoed to the door. At the door, as she was stepping out, she switched off the light. She closed the door very gently.

He lay in bed and listened to the click of her heels along

the street. After she had walked a few yards she began to run. Panic had seized her at the last moment.

When she was gone, he got out of bed and switched on the light. He went to his trousers and found the single one-pound note.

He grinned. He had scared her, all right. And she had reacted according to her kind. She wouldn't talk, not in years. Not until it was too late for her to do any harm. She would keep away from the police for a long time because she had the theft of money on her conscience. Her simple mind would not take into consideration the question of proof. If she accused him, he would accuse her; it would be as simple as that to her. She was fixed.

He thought that it was worth twenty-four pounds to get rid of her so easily and finally. What was twenty-four nicker, when tomorrow he was going to pick up a share of two hundred and fifty thousand?

*   *   *   *   *

Ella Bowie lay on her side, snug against the back of her own settee. Beside her, lying on his back, was Devery. He was not asleep; he was pensively smoking a cigarette. She realized that she had not asked him a single one of the questions she had intended to ask. She also realized that he had told her nothing. In fact, the affair had not gone at all according to plan. She had led him on, all right, but then he had taken her by storm. She had fallen into her own trap. It was not that he was an experienced lover. Quite the contrary, she thought. But he had a sexual dominance which was infinitely satisfying. She just had to go along with him. Even now, when he was quiet, the thought of him stirred her. She admitted to herself that she was infatuated with him. She reflected that she had never thought she would fall for a copper.

She raised herself on one elbow, and looked at the clock. "Ow!" she said. Then: "Would you like a drink? Or shall I make some supper?"

Her face was over his, and near. He smiled up at her. "Coffee, please," he said.

"Move your great feet then, and let me get out."

He moved his feet and legs, and sat up. She also sat up. She was naked except for a dressing-gown, and the gown was open. She did not care about that. She knew that scarred though her face might be, her body was sweet and clean and faultless.

"You're a smasher," he said, and kissed her.

She pulled the dressing-gown around her, and got up to make coffee. She asked: "Will you be going when you've had this?"

"Very likely," he said. "Though there's no great hurry."

She went to him and put her arms round his neck. Standing beside him as he sat, she pressed his head to her bosom. "Don't go yet," she whispered.

*　　*　　*　　*　　*

The Plumber was also reclining. It was a big, modern settee, but it had an old-fashioned arrangement at one end: the arm would let down so that a tall man could lie full length upon it. He lay full length. On the table within easy reach there were drinks and cigarettes. The room was warm.

The girl beside him was small and neatly built, and pretty. No more than pretty. He thought about that. She was a little Miss Prim really. One of the quiet ones, as the saying went. Normally a man like himself would not have looked twice at her. It had been a whim, a momentary aberration, which had made him make love to her in the first place. And then he found that he had lit a fire. It was amazing. That slight body of hers was a furnace of passion. When she was near him her attraction for him was irresistible. It was a fact, he could not leave her alone. And she was mad about him.

Her jealousy was some indication of her feeling for him. She had answered his telephone one day when a woman friend called him. Her remarks to the woman had ended *that* affair, with certainty. But she had still been furiously jealous, and she had tried to do a foolish and dangerous thing.

The foolishness, he admitted, had also been partly due to her Miss Prim mentality. She wanted him to end his criminal career. She thought that he had made enough money. She wanted him to take her away, and marry her. Marriage had not been mentioned, but he knew that it was in her mind. Miss Prim.

She had gone out in a flaring temper, threatening that she would stop his merry canter. He had let her go, not believing her. He had had to let her go anyway, because it had been time for him to go out and make a telephone contact with MacFarlane. His own phone was not used for business except in the most dire emergency.

When he had made his contact from a public phone box not far away, MacFarlane mentioned that he had just seen the girl. Going somewhere in a hurry, Mac had remarked. And in the general direction of Police Headquarters. "Get after her, Alex," had been the command. "Stop her at any cost."

After giving that order, the Plumber remembered, he had been deucedly uneasy. MacFarlane was a murderous little brute. He would stop her, if he had to kill her to do it. If he did kill her, it would be a calamity. Her death would naturally lead the police to her family, and young Blundell was her brother. Starting with Blundell, the police might begin to put two and two together. Furthermore, and worse, the girl's picture would be in the paper, and nosy neighbours who had seen her going to and fro might tell the police of her connexion with himself, the Plumber. That would mean two gaolbirds having a connexion with one murder case. The police would not regard that as a mere coincidence. They would move along from there, all right. The girl's death was something which could not be afforded.

But it had all ended harmlessly. Hannah had been in the offing, 'dogging out' for MacFarlane while he made his call. Mac had signalled him. They had taken a taxi and caught up with the girl. Apparently she had cooled off enough to see the folly of going to the police station, because they saw her enter a phone box. She made a brief call, and they met her as she stepped out of the box. She knew them both, and she did not struggle when they took her to some quiet backyard around there. She refused to tell them anything about her phone call. Mac struck her, and searched her bag. She still refused to talk, and Mac struck her again. He probably enjoyed doing that, the little devil. The worst might have happened then, but somehow she got away. She ran out of the yard and got to the main street, where they dared not touch her. They had to let her go.

Mac was a smart little character, one had to admit. He had told the girl what would happen to her if she played the grasshopper, and he had decided that temporarily there was no more danger from her. But he suspected that there would be a return call, and he waited near the phone box while Hannah scouted around to make sure that the box wasn't under police surveillance. Some man called the box, some cagey type who was not fooled by Mac's attempt to talk like a woman. The man pretended that he was calling some place called Cleary's.

Well, it all came out eventually. She was sent for and she came, with a swollen mouth and a black eye. She was only a little defiant, saying that the next job had better be called off, because she had informed the police of the place and the time. Later she admitted that she had not told the police anything, though she had indeed intended to stop the next job. No more than that. She swore that she would not have given the police any other information.

Whether or not her story was strictly true, the girl could not be killed. And if she could not be killed she had to be brought back to the fold, and made safe there. He had lectured her, and she had been contrite. He had told her that she was the only woman for him, and she had wept. After that he had made her an accomplice. She had carried messages and 'cased' jobs for him. She was involved. She dared not talk for her own sake. In any case, he thought, she was safe enough so long as he kept off other women.

Eventually she had told him that the policeman she had tried to contact was one Detective Sergeant Devery. She had seen him in court at the time of her brother's trial, and she had asked someone who he was. Then, wishing to speak to a policeman, she had asked for him. Because he had the sort of face she liked! Could you beat it! Women!

She was content enough now, because the next job would

be the last one. She knew now that her indiscretion might easily have ruined everything. If the police had spotted her! Phew! Come to think of it, women were dangerous creatures. Illogical, emotional, and impulsive.

He thought of the famous men of the past to whom women had brought disaster. Samson, Mark Antony, Marat, Parnell. Those were all he could think of at the moment, though there must be hundreds. There was, he mused whimsically, also Robert Connor, the prominent Granchester solicitor. A woman had brought disaster to him, too.

But this woman would cause nobody's downfall. That danger had been averted. One more job, and he would take her away for a holiday. But they would not go to where he kept his boat. She did not know about the boat. That was his private form of transport in an emergency.

They would go to France or Spain or Italy; the best hotels; that sort of holiday. That was what she wanted. How long would he keep her with him? He did not know.

Sometime he would leave her, but when that happened she would not again go running to Detective Sergeant Devery. For acting as messenger, and as look-out, and as a harmless-looking scout who reconnoitred his targets for robbery, she had accepted her share of the plunder. She wasn't Miss Prim enough to refuse the wherewithal to buy a mink coat. She was in it up to the neck, and so was her brother. She would never talk.

In any case, it did not matter. When he left her, he would assume a new identity in a new country. The police would never find him. Getaways were his speciality.

He thought about tomorrow's job, the big job. The big tickle, as Beadle called it. It would go as smoothly and a good deal more quietly than a civic ball. This time he would not have a fire or a fake burglary to draw the police in another direction. They would now be wise to that move. No, he would go straight to the objective, and in. Once he was in, the job was done. After he was in, nothing could go wrong, because of the getaway. It was a lulu. The best yet. Even if the police were right on his heels, they would be fooled.

They would think that he had evaporated into the night air, and his men with him.

"What are you thinking about?" the girl asked.

"You, sweetheart," he replied. "Paris, Biarritz, San Sebastian, the Riviera, the Costa Brava."

"Capri," she said.

"Positano."

"Venice."

"Taormina."

"Where's that?"

"It's in Sicily."

"Ooh!" She snuggled against him. "It'll be lovely. It'll be like a honeymoon."

"I wouldn't be surprised," he answered.

It was about time, he reflected. He could just about hold the men together for one more job. They hadn't much sense. Several of them were primed for an outburst: their money was burning the linings of their pockets. When they began to squander their money, the police would get to know. And some of them had been badly shaken by that fellow Martineau hanging about in a disguise. What were four of them doing in one pub, the idiots? Fortunately they had not actually been talking together. Probably no real harm had been done. But it was high time the business was wrapped up.

What would the robins do then, poor things? Carew would be all right. He was going to make a new start in Rhodesia. He had it all laid on; papers and a new identity. He would do all right in Africa, with his style and accent, and a sufficiency of money. Beadle yearned for his home town, the Big Smoke. Aldgate Pump. He was a fool if he went there. The Metropolitan Police would pick him up. However, that would not matter to anyone else, because Beadle would never talk. Whitehead showed sense. He was going to lie low, and then buy a new taxi, and after an interval another, until he had a small fleet and a nice business. Novak was going to Canada, where he had some relations. How he was going to get his money there was his own affair. Flint was going to breed running dogs in a big way. Ah well, every man to his own fancy. The other five, what were their ambitions, if any? The Plumber did not know, and he did not care.

The girl stirred beside him. She gently nipped the lobe of his ear.

"We'll go by air, darling," he said.

*   *   *   *   *

It was very late when Devery walked home. As he went along he reflected that it had been quite an evening. A sinful but satisfactory evening. With regard to that, he argued that he had nothing on his conscience. He was quite unattached, and so, morally, was the woman. No third person had been hurt, or betrayed, or dishonoured. A man had to have a bit of fun sometimes.

Still, he hoped that Martineau had not been wanting him for anything. He hoped that the Plumber had not been active. He did not want to have to tell Martineau that he had been engaged in dalliance.

Ella had asked him to come again, tomorrow night. Well, tonight really, since this was morning. He had promised, conditionally. The job came first. This might be the Plumber's night. He wanted to be in at the kill, if there was a kill. He thought that he would have done more than anybody to bring it about.

Cherchez la femme. The old, old story. Everything started with the Blundell girl. It was all due to her, and to his own persistence in continuing to seek her, and his luck in seeing her. The Farways idea came indirectly from her. Allott, Cooper, Straw, Thompson, they had all been Farways graduates, but they had all been chronic wrongdoers moving in a small, familiar orbit. One expected them to be in mischief, and one did not associate the prison with their criminal background. But that was not the case with Owen Blundell. He was of a different type. It was Blundell who really brought the idea that Farways Prison was the incubator which had hatched the Plumber's gang, and it was Farways which had provided the list of suspects.

111

'That wench was a bit of luck for me,' Devery said to himself. 'I wonder if I shall ever know what she was going to tell me when she phoned Headquarters."

CHAPTER TWELVE

THOUGH most of his suspects, or their homes, were under observation from sunset to sunrise on Thursday night, Martineau was relieved when they made no move. If they had gone out on a job he would have been able to do something about it, but not in the comprehensive, sure-fire way in which he intended to do it on Friday, when everything would be ready.

At his conference with the senior officers of the force, he asked for men and transport; a lot of transport and a lot of men, and all the men experienced detectives. The Chief pointed out that he could be mistaken.

"You have no real evidence," he said. "You might be barking up the wrong tree. I can't strip the town of men just because of an idea."

Martineau had given up trying to tell the Chief that he was *not* barking up the wrong tree. "Very well, sir," he replied. "I'll lower my sights. Can you spare me six plain cars and thirty men, and all the walkie-talkies we've got? I'd like to have a detective sergeant in charge of each car."

The Chief pondered, and then he nodded. "That's reasonable enough, I suppose. You can have them. For the security of the town I'll make my own dispositions."

"I'd like twenty-four of my men to be armed, sir. And I'd like all the regular motor-patrol officers to be armed. If anything happens, some of them are sure to get into the thick of it."

"Very well, but I'd like to know where we're going to get so many pistols and revolvers. I'm not having you disarming my emergency squads."

The Assistant Chief Constable spoke up. "We have one hundred brand-new Enfield forty-fives, sir," he said. "We've had them since the invasion crisis of nineteen-forty."

"So many? I thought they'd gone back."

"No, sir. The rifles were returned to the War Office, but not the revolvers."

"But we've had them sixteen or seventeen years! Brand new, indeed! What condition are they in?"

"In first class condition, sir. They've been regularly cleaned and oiled, and the ammunition has been properly stored. I was looking at it only last week."

"Very well. Issue every gun we have. Let Martineau take what he needs, and issue the remainder to men who know how to use them."

"Every man knows how to use a gun, sir. The older men were trained by me during the war. All the younger men have served in the armed forces."

"Well, well," said the Chief, a little put out by all this precise information. "Issue the guns as you think fit, then."

The Chief went on to outline his own plans for security. Wealthy people had been publicly advised not to keep large sums of money at home, but to lodge them at their banks. The same advice had been given to the managers of big shops and stores, and business premises where large sums of money were handled. All jewellers' shops, furriers' shops and banks were to be specially guarded by police. The main office of the Granchester Economic Society, a co-operative concern which was holding a quarter of a million pounds in readiness to pay out in dividends to its members, was already picketed by armed policemen. To guard against diversions of the sort which had resulted in the burning of Sir Clement Wesley's warehouse, there were two emergency squads waiting at Headquarters. One squad could go to the diversion, if any, and the second squad was ready to go to the scene of the real crime wherever it occurred. It did not seem possible for the Plumber to commit another crime and get away with a worthwhile amount of plunder.

Martineau listened to the Chief, and was content. He had got almost as much as he wanted, and he was confident that before daylight on Saturday his own arrangements would be the ones which would bring results. As soon as darkness fell on Friday he would have four prime suspects marked down: Blundell, Bowie, the ex-lawyer Connor, and MacFarlane. Also under observation would be Bernard Flint, of Churlham, and Tom Egan. Flint had a bad record, he was on the Farways short list, and he did not appear to be working for a living. Egan, who had been inactive for the last week or two, was watched as a precaution. Stanislaus (Stanley) Novak lived in the neighbouring borough of Boyton, outside the jurisdiction of the Granchester police. Rather than bring the Boyton police into the job, Martineau left Novak alone.

Of the others, Beadle and Carew were still in hiding, and John Hannah had vanished. On the day of Martineau's unmasking at Jimmy Ganders, Hannah had changed his lodgings, and his new abode had not yet been located. And yet, as it turned out, Hannah's part in the next Plumber job was going to cause him more anxiety than any other single factor.

Ten men made a big enough housebreaking gang, in all conscience, but Martineau reminded himself that there would be other members whom he did not know. There would be reserves, such as Egan. There would be one or two good drivers in addition to Carew. There might be messengers and contact men. And finally there was the fence, who was perhaps the most important criminal of them all. The man who buys stolen jewels is the capitalist of crime. Without him, the wheels of that dangerous industry would not turn.

By Friday afternoon Martineau had chosen his men and gathered his equipment. He called a conference of his six sergeants in his own office. He had chosen all his men carefully, but he had been particularly careful with the sergeants. With the exception of Devery, whose choice was automatic, he had preferred stolid men to excitable ones, whatever their brains or ability. "We'll have no mistakes," he told them. "If one of you happens to lose touch with his client through being too cautious, I don't grumble. But any man who gets himself spotted and gives our game away, he goes back into uniform tomorrow. And that goes for your men; you can tell them so. The main thing is, use your wits and keep your distance until you are instructed to close in and make an arrest."

Adequately briefed, Martineau's men took up their stations at nightfall. Each car crew had the permanent or temporary address of one man, and at least two officers in each car personally knew the man. He was their 'client'. Also, each of Martineau's detectives personally knew four or more of the ten suspects. And each man had spent some time studying the photographs—full figure, full face, and profile —of those suspects which he did not know. The Plumber's men went masked about their business, but unmasked they would be immediately known.

Each of Martineau's six cars was radio-equipped, and he also had six rooftop observers with field radio sets and nigh' glasses. These latter men were not armed. Their job was cold, dreary, and unexciting, but most important. They had the consolation of knowing that they were considered to be the most reliable men, with the best eyesight.

On that Friday evening, Caps Bowie went out long before dark, for the simple reason that he was too restless to stay in. He was under orders to take no liquor, which he interpreted as meaning that he must take not more than three or four drinks, so he went to a cinema. The main feature was a film which had been well received; everyone said that it was good. Bowie could not get interested in it. He had too much on his mind. He thought about tomorrow's wealth, more money than he had ever dreamed of possessing. He also thought about his wife. Had she received his letter? How would she take it? Would she reply? Would he have to wait for days and days consumed with impatience while she made up her mind to reply? The mere prospect of such a wait brought him to his feet. He could no longer sit and watch make-believe. He left the cinema and went to a billiard hall.

In the billiard hall—NO GAMBLING ALLOWED—Bowie got into a game of snooker with a twenty-year-old shark who

115

took three pounds from him in three successive games. Normally Caps was a very good player. In a sober and settled game he would have taken money from the youth, but tonight he played wildly. He tried to concentrate, and missed chances which at another time he could have taken with the wrong end of the cue. As he paid over the third one-pound note he suddenly realized what was the matter with him. He needed a drink.

He went to Jimmy Ganders, and he was relieved to find that none of his companions of tonight's adventure was present. He had a stiff whisky, and felt a little better. He also remembered his orders. His second drink was a pint of beer.

In Jimmy Ganders he was found by four friends; Ned Higgs, Bert Sloan, Sammy Orpington. and Wally Waters. They greeted him with normal friendliness, as if the meeting were purely accidental—as everyone except Ned Higgs thought it was. He bought them beer, but did not have his own glass filled up. "I've been drinking a long while, and the night's young," he said.

They accepted the explanation, and he was content to remain with them until closing time. The talk was almost exclusively about football. There would be many league matches on the following day, and teams were beginning to settle down into the season's form. It all passed the time for Caps. He lost that keyed-up feeling.

Nevertheless, he continued to drink sparingly. Ned Higgs was aware that he was drinking sparingly. All the time he was aware of Caps. But everyone was perfectly friendly.

At closing time, Waters invited them all to his home for supper and a game of cards. This seemed to be a good idea to everyone except Bowie, normally a keen gambler. "Leave me out," he said.

His friends stared at him. "What's up with you, Caps?" Orpington wanted to know.

"Got a woman to see."

"She must be a warm 'un if she can keep you away from a poker game," Sloan remarked with a grin.

116

"Well, come and have your supper, anyway," urged Waters hospitably. "Then you can go and see your woman."

"Supper's laid on," said Caps. "Thanks all the same, Wally."

"This woman must be summat special," said Higgs, narrow-eyed but still quite friendly. "You've been taking your drink very steady."

Caps shrugged. "I'm not in form for it. To tell you the truth, I'm in two minds about going straight home to bed, and to hell with the woman."

When he said that, Higgs knew definitely that he was lying. Like other liars, he had failed to stick to a good story. He had changed his mind, and changed his tale for one which might explain his unusual abstemiousness. If he did not feel well, he might really fail to keep an appointment with a girl. In that case, he would join the poker party if he could. No slight indisposition would ever keep Caps away from a good game of cards. Therefore something else was keeping him away; something important.

"Ah well," said Waters, "I dare say we'll manage without you. Good night, lad."

Talking, the group of men had walked out of the public house. Bowie made his adieux and went away in the direction of his furnished room. The other four men sauntered away towards the district where Waters lived. But as soon as they were round the first corner, Higgs stopped. The others also stopped.

"You'll have to play three-hand, lads," said Higgs. "I've got a job to do for Dixie. You're my alibi. Don't forget, I'm having supper at Wally's place and playing poker till three o'clock in the morning. We start playing at about eleven-thirty. About one o'clock we start playing stud. Break up sometime between three and half-past, you didn't notice particular. It'll be no use telling the cops we played for cigarette cards, so you'll make a reluctant admission: Wally's about holding his own, Bert and Sammy are a few bob in pocket, so you think I must have lost about fifteen bob. Is that all clear?"

"We'll play that way and reckon you're with us," said

Waters. "Half eleven to one, one to three. And don't forget the hand where I got four knaves."

Higgs left them then, and hurried after Bowie. He guessed that wherever the man intended to go, he was first going home.

But in his hurry Higgs was circumspect. He did not want to be spotted at the outset. Where a street was deserted he ran a-tiptoe from corner to corner, but at each corner he stopped, and looked and listened.

Because he was careful he saw a car hidden snugly a short distance from Bowie's place. The occupants of the car did not see him, because it is difficult to see a fractional part of a man's face as he looks round a corner at night. He retreated, and made a detour, and approached the car from behind. He still only showed a small part of his face as he studied it. He was patient. He watched for small movements, and presently he was reasonably sure that there were three men in the car. They were heavy-shouldered men who sat high in their seats. Cops!

Higgs withdrew from the corner, and stood for a moment considering. Could he get near to Bowie's place without being seen by the policeman who was undoubtedly watching it? He visualized the layout of buildings in the area, and thought that it could be done.

Opposite the end of the short street of shabby houses where Bowie lived, there was a small cotton mill. Higgs circled in that direction, approaching the mill yard from the safe side. There were a few people about, returning home from their evening's excursions. None of them were interested in him, but he waited until there was no one in sight before he climbed over the gate of the mill yard.

Across the yard, close to the wall on the side overlooking Bowie's place, was the tall chimney stack of the mill. Its base rose out of the ground near the boiler house. Higgs thought that if he could find something to stand on, he could take up a position with his back to the chimney, and see over the wall without showing a silhouette. He crossed the yard, walking quietly. He had started to go around the base of the chimney when a slight, brief sound stopped him. It was a sound like the creak of a complaining floorboard. Someone had shifted his position on an empty skep or weft box, on the other side of the chimney.

Higgs had to be sure. He edged round the chimney until he could just see the man. A tall fellow whom he did not recognize was looking over the wall in the direction of Bowie's place. Higgs silently retreated, moving to flank and rear so that he could observe the watcher from a distance. He found a pile of old skeps and took cover behind them.

The night was clear and cool and starry, and quiet. There was no moon, and no wind. There were not many people stirring in that part of town, and few cars could be heard. Higgs would have liked a cigarette but he was afraid that it might make him want to cough. He did not have a cigarette. A distant church clock chimed the quarter hour. Eleven fifteen.

The night became even more quiet. The clock announced the half hour, and the three quarters. Higgs told himself that he was pretty well browned off of this waiting game. Then the man he was watching went over the wall.

Higgs ran to the chimney and climbed on to the box. The tall man was running along the street. He stopped at the corner and looked round it. Then he looked back. Higgs heard a car. It was the car with the three men in it. It went slowly along the street as the man at the other end disappeared.

Higgs decided not to follow. It was too dangerous. If he got too near, the police might arrest him when they arrested Bowie, if they were going to arrest Bowie. Also, there were aspects of the affair which he did not understand, and his lack of understanding made him nervous. Not knowing that there was another watcher on the roof of the mill he wondered how the man following Bowie had managed to call up the police car, which had been a hundred and fifty yards away around two corners. Did he have a wireless set in his pocket, or summat? The cops seemed to have all sorts of gadgets nowadays.

Higgs went in search of a public telephone box, but he also went in the direction of Dixie Costello's flat. Ten minutes' fast walking brought him to a phone, and then he was only five minutes' walk from Dixie's place. Nevertheless, he used the phone.

The girl called Popsie answered the phone. "This is Ned. I want Dixie," said Higgs without preamble. Popsie put down the phone without comment, and Dixie came on the line. "Well?" he asked.

Higgs told him about Bowie's behaviour during the evening, and about the police car and the watcher. "Wherever he's gone, they're on his tail," he concluded.

Dixie swore. Then he said: "Come up."

When Higgs arrived at the flat, Dixie was alone. "I sent Popsie out with the car, to get Waddy and Pete and the Dog," he explained. "We've got work to do tonight. I hope we have, at any rate. It should have been done before."

"What sort of work?"

"If the bogies don't pick up Caps, we're going to do him," the boss mobster growled. Higgs looked at him, and saw that he was the Dixie of old; the nerveless, ruthless, indomitable man of the fighting days.

"You mean—do him proper?" queried Higgs, suddenly chilled.

Dixie nodded. "I'm not asking you to do what I won't do myself. I'll be with you. I'll do it personally, in fact."

"We've known Caps a long while. Do we *have* to kill him?"

"Yes."

"For God's sake, why?"

"Because we've known him a long while. And he's known us. If he gets picked up with this other crowd, there's going to be some murder raps floating around. Four, to be precise. Scaffolding jobs, you understand? Caps will be sweated proper. They'll dangle the rope in front of his nose. Do you think he'll care what he says about you and me when he's trying to duck out of a murder job? They'll ask him, you know. They'll go back years. That old bastard Clay has been wanting to get at me for a long time. And so has Martineau."

"Caps wouldn't shop us."

"He's deceived us, hasn't he? So you can't say he's dead

120

loyal. Would you lay seven years of your life to nothing that he won't shop us?"

Higgs was silent.

"We've been in some middling dodgy doings in our time, Ned," said Dixie more gently. "I don't need to count 'em off on my fingers and toes for you."

Higgs sighed. "You're the boss," he conceded. "What's the griff?"

"You know where Century Works is," said Dixie, suddenly businesslike.

"The chemical place, yes."

"In the yard at the back there's a big tank. It's been there since I was a kid. It's full of sulphuric acid."

"You're sure there's acid in it now?"

"Yes. Sloan's brother told me. He works there. The planks across the top of the tank are fastened down by two big padlocks. Waddy won't have any trouble with those. He'll unlock 'em and hide in a corner and look out for stray cops. When we've done, he'll lock up after us."

"How are we going to get hold of Caps?"

"We'll picket his place. You, me, Pete and the Dog. If the police don't get him, we do. We treat him gentle, till we get him to Century Works. Then out he goes, like a light, and we put him into his nice warm bath. Nobody will ever find hide or hair of him. The bogies will think he's gone to America."

Higgs went to the sideboard and poured himself a stiff whisky. He thought about the alibi he had arranged. It had been merely a precaution. He had not expected it to be an alibi for murder.

There were sounds of entry, and feet on the stairs. Popsie entered the room with three men. Waddy was a plump little fellow with quick, darting eyes. Pete was an ex-prizefighter, and he looked it. The man known as the Dog was huge and loose-limbed. He had the melancholy eyes, long lip, and sagging jowl of a bloodhound.

CHAPTER THIRTEEN

WHEN Caps Bowie left home at eleven forty-five that night he was followed by the detective sergeant who had had the doubtful honour of arresting him for slashing his wife. The sergeant knew Bowie well. He could pick him out in a crowd by merely seeing the hunch of his thick shoulders and the set of his head. He had no difficulty in following him in the dark. It was much easier than daylight shadowing. He kept his distance, following Martineau's instruction to lose his 'client' rather than be spotted by him. Bowie stopped once or twice, pretending to look into a darkened shop window but in reality looking back to see if he was being followed. When Bowie stopped, the sergeant immediately froze, close to the wall, using even a very slight projection for cover. In the dark, Bowie could not discern him.

Bowie reached a cross-roads and turned the corner as if he were about to go in a north-easterly direction. Again the sergeant froze, watching anxiously. Bowie might be standing at the corner, peeping. He might stand and peep for several minutes, or he might be walking rapidly away. The sergeant slipped into a doorway and waited. Far behind, the police car stopped also. The men in the car could not see the sergeant at all, except when he showed his 'tail light'. That is to say, he put his fingers over the glass of his torch and flashed it towards them occasionally. There was no glare, but the light showed bright pink between his fingers.

At last the sergeant decided to risk going to the corner. He stepped out of his doorway and went forward boldly, in the middle of the sidewalk. When he reached the corner there was nobody in sight. This was a main road, wide and straight, but neither a car nor a pedestrian moved upon it

"Dammit, I've lost him," the sergeant said bitterly.

Then in the distance he saw the lights of an approaching car. He slipped into the first shop doorway. He was not going to be seen by the occupants of any strange car tonight. He turned up the collar of his dark suit and put his hands in his pockets. He hunched, so that the pale blur of his face would not be seen. The car went by, slowed, and pulled over. It stopped at the kerb a hundred yards away. Bowie walked out of the darkened entrance of a small cinema and got into the car. It sped away.

The sergeant slipped round the corner with his torch in his hand. He flashed it continuously and urgently. His car came up at speed. The sergeant got into the seat beside the driver.

"Good," he said contentedly as the car, running without lights, swung out into the main road. "We can just see his tail lights. Now it's up to you, driver."

* * * * *

The detective sergeant in charge of the car which was to follow Owen Blundell was the sergeant who had arrested him for larceny and falsification of accounts less than two years before. For this reason, the sergeant took the precaution of wearing some horn-rimmed spectacles without lenses, on the principle that any disguise is better than none. He picked up Blundell when he left home early in the evening and went to a dance hall. He noted with faint excitement that the young man was wearing a very dark suit and no hat. Probably, the sergeant thought, he had a dark cap or beret in his pocket. He was wearing dark suede shoes with very thick crepe-rubber soles. The sergeant, whose experience of jive and bebop was somewhat limited, could not see for the life of him how a fellow could dance in shoes like that. He thought that the business of going into the dance hall might be a subterfuge. Blundell was dressed for creeping around in the dark, and not for dancing. He had every exit watched, but Blundell stayed in the dance hall until half-past eleven. When he emerged, the sergeant followed him. And all the time the sergeant wondered how a narrow-gutted, chinless fancy boy like that could summon up the courage to do his part in a real neck-or-nothing job. How on earth had Martineau spotted this one?

Blundell walked for some distance, in a north-easterly direction. He looked behind him occasionally, but he did not see the sergeant. At about eleven forty-five he disappeared into the shadowed entrance of a small repertory theatre. Apparently he was early for his appointment. It was nearly midnight when a car came and stopped at the theatre. He skipped light-footed to the kerb and got into a rear seat. As the car was driven away the sergeant called up his own car. Before he could get into it he was passed by another car, which was running without lights at a discreet distance behind Blundell's vehicle.

"Well, well!" the sergeant said. "It's a perishing procession."

* * * * *

Devery was in charge of the car which was to follow the astute and dangerous MacFarlane. Martineau had chosen him specially for this difficult assignment. "He'll probably give you the slip," the chief inspector had warned. "Never mind if he does, just as long as he doesn't suspect he's being tailed."

That was the point which Martineau had hammered home time and time again. "Whatever you do, don't be spotted. Remember they'll all be as jumpy as show ponies."

Devery's task was indeed difficult. Besides being naturally alert, Alex MacFarlane was full of suspicion. His mind was able to dwell upon possibilities, because now he had no girl to engage his attention with her chatter. Also, during the evening he was lonely and restless, and he wandered from place to place, always sober and always watchful.

Having to keep an eye on him, Devery reflected that he did the damnedest things. Sometimes it seemed that the man knew he was being followed. He went into pubs by the front door and quitted them by the back door. He went into cafés and then stood staring out of the window. And worst of all, he sometimes seemed to change his mind in the street, turning about and retracing his steps. It was impossible to trail him discreetly on foot, and Devery soon gave up trying. He called up his car, and got into a rear seat. The men in the front seats were young out-division detectives whom MacFarlane did not know.

At last Devery decided that the business of shadowing MacFarlane at all was much too dangerous. The little Scot even had a habit of stopping in his tracks and turning, and standing there until he had had a good look at every moving vehicle in the street. A car which was crawling along behind him would be suspect, even though it was some distance away. The first time that happened, the police car was fortunately near the entrance to a side street, and the young man at the wheel had the wit to make the turn, so that he appeared to have been slowing up for the corner. The second time it happened, the car was opposite the entrance to the Northland Hotel. "Pull in and stop," ordered Devery. "Everyone except the driver remain perfectly still."

"Now," the sergeant went on. "He can't see anybody in the car at that distance if there's no movement. You get out, driver, and keep your knees bent so you don't look tall enough for a bobby. Walk round the car and kick the tyres. Then go into the pub and have a drink. Be about ten minutes. Walk with your knees bent when you come out."

The driver did as he was told, and went into the Northland. The other three men remained motionless in the car. The distant figure of MacFarlane was still standing there, and his face could be seen. He seemed to be looking straight at the police car.

"If we get away with this, it's the last chance we take," said Devery. "I never saw such a man. If he turns back, we've had it."

MacFarlane did not turn back, but he stood for a good five minutes looking towards the car. Inside the car there was no movement at all. He turned and walked about twenty yards, then stopped and turned again. Then, apparently satisfied, he went on his way.

"Let him go," said Devery, greatly relieved. "We'll pick him up later."

He was able to laugh at his driver when that young man walked solemnly out of the hotel like a man with crippled knees. He wondered if Ella was busy. She would have to go home by herself tonight. Or at least, she wouldn't be going home with one Devery.

One circumstance made Devery fairly confident that he would be able to pin a tail on to MacFarlane later in the evening. The Scotsman was wearing a light grey sports coat and flannels, and it was extremely likely that he would go home and change into dark clothes before he set out upon any errand of serious mischief. In fact, the sergeant told himself, it had been a foolish and dangerous waste of time to attempt to follow such a man at all until the last crucial hour.

He had developed so much respect for his client's perspicacity that he did not go within a quarter of a mile of the man's place of abode. He relied upon his roof-top observer, who in this case was not on a roof but among the higher branches of a large beech tree in the garden of what had once been a vicarage, diagonally across the street from MacFarlane's place and in plain view of it. It was as well for Devery that experience had taught him to keep his distance. The observer reported that before he went indoors at eleven o'clock MacFarlane made a tour of the area, nosing into doorways and into the vicarage garden. He stood at the foot of the beech tree and peered up into the darkness, but he did not use a torch. The observer was glad to be able to report that the suspicious little scoundrel had gone up to his room, drawn the curtain, and put on the light.

"Now he's turned out the light," said the observer twenty minutes later. "But he hasn't appeared yet. He'll be standing in the dark, looking out of the window."

There was silence for nearly ten minutes, then the announcer said: "Can you beat it? There's a damn big tomcat climbed up here! I think it likes my company. It's purring away like an electric shaver." Then almost immediately: "He's away! MacFarlane I mean! He dodged along the street like a shadow. He's gone now, towards Sutcliffe Street. He's all yours. And boy, you can have him!"

Devery picked up MacFarlane as he emerged from Sutcliffe Street. But he was too cautious and his client was too slippery. In five minutes he had lost him again. Instead of blundering around in search of him he wisely stayed where he was. He sat in the car waiting for news and while he waited the thought crossed his mind that Ella would now be sound asleep in bed, he hoped. Then came news which sent him away at speed, with concealment no longer necessary, and with no time to think about women.

* * * * *

At half-past eleven Ella Bowie ceased to hope. She knew that Devery would not come to her that night. He would be busy, out after the Granchester Gang, as the newspapers now called it. It was a pity, because she had some information for him. It was in a letter from the man she hated. She thought that it was highly incriminating. Caps Bowie had money, thousands of pounds. And it was stolen money. That was why nobody had ever heard of it. If Caps had won it on the horses he would have bragged about it from the start. All the town would have known it, and half the county as well. Why did he have a dozen bank accounts? Because he was afraid of some bank clerk getting curious. He was a thief, a member of the Gang. For some time she had suspected, and now she was sure.

She stopped in the act of undressing. He might even be guilty of murder! If she could get him put away for that, vengeance would be sweet indeed. It would almost be as sweet as that other vengeance which she had been planning for years.

There was the risk, of course. The penalty for chattering was the long silence of the grave, if it became known that she was the one who had given information. Could she trust Devery to handle the matter in such a way that no one would ever know? She thought that she could. She could not be sure, yet, that he was in love with her, but she knew that he liked her. He would see that no harm came to her.

There was also the question of reward. She had seen in the papers that insurance companies had offered rewards for information which would lead to the recovery of stolen property. Devery might even arrange for her to get a reward.

Tomorrow she would tell him. Tomorrow, everything would be going her way. And tomorrow night Devery would be here, with her.

* * * * *

The crew of men who were concerned with the welfare of Bernard Flint had a very simple job. Flint lived in Churlham, where many identical streets of blackened brick dwelling-houses branched from the Churlham Road like the rungs of a single-stemmed burglar's ladder. Alma Street, where Flint lived with a sluttish wife and a neglected family, was distinguished from the rest only by its handy situation. It was so handy that Mrs. Flint had been known to boast that sometimes a fortnight went by without her having to walk farther than the corner. For on the corner, meaning of course the four corners where Alma Street crossed the Churlham Road, were the Tivoli Cinema, the Shamrock Inn, the Tivoli Fisheries (Frying To-Nite! Only the Finest Faroe Haddock! !), and a big multiple grocery store which sold butcher's meat as well. It was a very handy place. The police thought so too. They were able to put an observer high on the roof of the cinema. He was so high that he could see the front door of Flint's house and also the backyard gate.

It was easy to see Flint when he emerged from his house half an hour before midnight, because the streets of Churlham were practically deserted at that time. He walked straight to the corner, crossed the road, and vanished under the canopy at the cinema entrance. When he vanished, only one circumstance prevented the observer from getting into a panic and calling up his sergeant. Flint had crossed the road not as if he intended to walk along the other side, but as if he were going into the cinema. That was strange, because the cinema had been closed and in darkness for twenty minutes or more. While the observer was pondering about that, a car stopped at the kerb below and Flint got into it. The rest was easy, for the observer.

The sergeant in charge of the car which was put on Flint's trail was interested to note that it stopped no fewer than three times, and each time near the entrance to a theatre or cinema. If that meant that three more men had been picked up, then there were at least five men in the car. Presently he learned that there were three more police cars following him; far, far back. He remarked over the radio that it was a blooming procession. "Yes, sarge," the clerk at Headquarters answered wearily. That made three sergeants out of four who had said it was a procession.

*   *   *   *   *

The sergeant—an ambitious and pugnacious man—who had been detailed to watch Tom Egan had the easiest job of all. Apparently Egan was still on the Plumber's retired list. Early in the evening he went to the Prodigal Son and stayed there till closing time. Then he bought some fish and chips and ate them out of the wrapping paper as he walked home. At home, he went to bed, and he was in bed when the police went for him in the morning. From eleven o'clock until daylight the sergeant waited for him to move, and when the news of great events began to come over the police radio his mouth set in a bitter line. Fellow officers were in action, gaining credit, acquiring promotion, while he and his men had to sit there waiting and watching for a great hog of a man who was snoring in bed. And the waiting was obligatory. The sergeant's orders were inflexible upon that point. He waited, and quietly cursed Egan. The big, fat, lazy, thick-headed, drunken, dirty, thieving, murdering, stinking, slinking, treacherous, lily-livered. . . .

You can't please some people. Egan would have said: "There I was, sleeping the sleep of the angels, and Sergeant Casey didn't like it. What *did* he want me to do, I ask you? Go out and rob somebody? I tell you, once them fellers get against you, you've had it. They won't let you live an honest life."

*   *   *   *   *

Martineau himself was in charge of the observations upon Robert Connor, but he had a sergeant in his crew, to take charge if he were called elsewhere. He certainly intended

129

to be called elsewhere, if action started before Connor had made any move. He realized that some of his men would think that he 'had it both ways,' as bosses are often supposed to have. But he was the man who had devised Operation Plumber, and he was in charge of it, and he would have to take most of the blame if it failed. For those reasons he had to have a certain freedom of movement. Though he chose to watch Connor, he had a car and a driver waiting for him at Headquarters, and they waited for him alone.

For similar reasons he chose Connor as his client. There was a possibility that the operation might develop into a contest of wits and strength between the Plumber and himself. *If* Connor was a member of the Plumber's gang, then Martineau could think of no man more likely to be the Plumber himself. Thus he sat, figuratively, on Connor's doorstep, hoping for the doubtful pleasure of meeting the Plumber.

Connor's home was in a centrally situated district of fading gentility which still had a reputation for respectability. He lived in Park Terrace, a row of tall town houses which had very profitably been turned into comfortable flats, and across the road from the Terrace was a small public park. On the other side, facing the backs of Park Terrace, was a row of smaller houses, and one of these happened to be occupied by a constable of the Granchester force. Martineau supplied the constable with a field radio set and gave him the congenial task of watching Connor's back door from his own rear bedroom, while an observer in the park watched the front door. It was unlikely that Connor would use his back door, if he knew that a policeman lived anywhere near.

Martineau had too much respect for the enemy to put his observer in the shrubbery opposite Connor's door. He looked for a place farther back, and not opposite the door. The best place he could find was a shrub-covered mound, and he put his man there with his back to a tree.

It was a long wait, and Martineau was restless. He moved from his observer to his car, and prowled about generally. But he never went nearer to Connor's flat than the observer's position. The flat was on the third storey of the four-storey house, and there were lights in the windows. He assumed that Connor was there. He fervently hoped that his assumption was correct.

At twenty minutes to twelve Connor's light went out. Martineau was standing with his observer in the park. "Keep still," he warned. "He'll have a good look out of the window before he comes downstairs. And be careful with those night glasses. Don't catch any reflection from the street lights."

They waited, then the observer raised his glasses carefully. "He's downstairs, standing back in the doorway," he reported. "I can just see his face, like a blur."

Connor remained in the doorway for several minutes, apparently looking across at the park. Then he emerged, a tall, dark, silent figure, and walked along the street. Martineau moved on a parallel course, treading noiselessly on the asphalt paths of the park.

When he left his own street behind, Connor followed a zigzag route, left, right, left, right along by-streets, in the general direction to a main road. Martineau did not doubt that he occasionally stopped when he had turned a corner, to look back to see if he was being followed. So every time his man disappeared from sight Martineau had to turn back and run along a parallel street, getting to the other end just in time to get another glimpse of him. The police car, alerted by the observer, slowly followed his erratic course a street-length behind.

When he reached the main road—Bishopsgate, actually —Martineau had the same unnerving experience as his colleagues. He found that his man had vanished. He waited, full of doubt as to what he ought to do. Then a car came along at speed, and he got into hiding just in time. He heard the car stop, and he returned to the corner. He saw Connor emerge from the covered entrance of a pin-table arcade. He signalled his own car, and took the seat beside the driver. On the radio the news was beginning to come in, about other men, and—so it seemed at first—several other cars.

"The job is moving," he said with a sort of grim satisfaction. "And for once in a blue moon we seem to have guessed right."

At Headquarters, the Chief Constable admitted to Superintendent Clay that Martineau had been right. "Of course, sir," said Clay, to give the impression that he had never had a moment's doubt of his subordinate's rightness.

They were standing beside the big table map in the communication room. The Chief loved a map, and he was following the course of the operation with a sort of anxious pleasure. It was he who sorted out the true situation from a confusion of messages: that the Plumber was using only two cars. One of them was being trailed by Martineau, while the other was being followed by no fewer than four police cars.

CHAPTER FOURTEEN

THE car which picked up Robert Connor was a big Humber, and it was driven by Nigel Carew, escaped convict. In the car with him were Frank Beadle, escaped convict, and the Pole known as Stanley Novak. Beadle was a notorious peterman, or safeblower. Novak was down in police records as a textile worker, but in Lublin, whence he came, he had been a skilled locksmith. Caps Bowie, a man somewhat given to exaggeration, had once remarked that Novak could open a lock by breathing on it.

Though he was not the leader, the most experienced thief of them all was Beadle, and he had the true professional's abhorrence of violence. He refused to carry a gun, or a cosh, or a knuckle-duster. To him, race-course hooligans like Bowie were the lowest form of human life, and he would only associate with such men under duress. He was, in a way, under duress now. The Plumber had found him a good and comfortable hiding-place in Granchester since his escape, and had 'organized him into the money'. The Plumber was his only contact in the city, and until he was ready to go elsewhere he had to be the Plumber's man. After tonight's job the gang would break up by order, and Beadle thought that he would leave his hide-out and go south. He longed for London, the Smoke, his home town, but he was afraid to go to London. He thought that with capital he could be quite comfortable in Brighton, where his ineradicable Cockney accent would not be noticeable. Brighton, then, after tonight. He did not feel very good about tonight. These lunatics— that was how he thought of the Plumber's men—had pistols. They were going after a huge sum of money which was guarded by policemen. There might be murder done. Murder had been committed once before in Beadle's presence, but not the murder of a cop. Killing coppers was the surest indirect way of committing suicide that he knew. He did not like the idea at all. He sat glum and silent in the car.

The thoughts of Robert Connor, the Plumber, were pursuing a variant of the same theme. He was not gloomy. He did not think that any policeman would be killed; but if they were, what of it? There would be no clues. Everyone would wear masks and gloves, and there would be a clean getaway. Not a perfect crime, perhaps, but too perfect for any effective police work to be done. The joint had been cased thoroughly by himself, Novak, and Grace Blundell, separately and at different times. Only three policemen had been detached to guard a quarter of a million pounds. Two of them patrolled outside the building, and the third sat beside the safe. Beside the safe also would be two or three aged but possibly plucky watchmen of the regular staff. Wandering around the several surrounding warehouses of the concern would be other watchmen. They could be disposed of if and when they were seen. If they succeeded in raising an alarm, it would not matter. The getaway took care of that.

The Plumber knew where to find the money because he had been told about it, years before, by an official of the society, when he himself had been a solicitor with a spotless reputation. The procedure was always the same. The money was in the form of one-pound notes, ten-shilling notes, silver and copper, because the average dividend paid out to the many thousands of working-class members was about fifty shillings. (No fivers, the Plumber reflected contentedly. As hot money, five-pound notes could be a nuisance.) Because of its bulk, an ordinary safe was not used to store the money. The whole of it was put into a big book safe in the main office. There, under guard, the money was considered to be in no danger.

In the main office then, in a book safe. Beadle would make short work of that. Tomorrow, the pay-out would take place in a shabby little tavern in Darktown, and not in the many branch stores of the Granchester Economic Society. A hundred thousand thrifty housewives would be disappointed. There would be the devil to pay. The Plumber grinned in the darkness of the car.

Carew drove very steadily, for several reasons. In the first place, he was on a strict timetable, and he did not want to arrive at the meeting place too early; secondly, he did not want to attract attention; thirdly, Beadle was carrying, among other things, a small bottle of nitro-glycerine. Beadle said that the stuff was safe enough, handled properly. Carew did not believe what Beadle said.

The car was moving in a north-easterly direction, along a wide, straight road which led into a district of factories and warehouses. Big buildings towered in the night. Somewhere, on a roughly parallel course, Luke Whitehead was driving a car containing the Plumber's second team; the stiffs, the riff-raff, the hewers of wood and drawers of water; Blundell, Bowie, Flint and MacFarlane.

When he was nearing his destination, the Plumber lowered the side window of the car and looked back along the road. Almost immediately he saw a flash of movement, some distance away. He thought that it might have been made by street lights shining on the radiator or windscreen of a vehicle running without lights. He watched. Presently he discerned a car. It looked like a moving black shadow as it passed under a street light.

He made no comment: the others were nervous enough already. But a following car, without lights, could not be ignored. He was satisfied that he had not been followed from his home. Carew and Beadle had not been followed: they had come from their hide-out. It was unlikely that Novak had been followed: he had come from Boyton, beyond the city boundaries, and he had alighted from his bus at a street corner, and not at the terminus.

The Plumber decided that it was a police car, shadowing a car full of men as a speculative venture. That did not matter, so long as his own driver could lose them for five minutes.

"Put on speed," he said. That was one way of finding whether or not the other car was deliberately following.

Carew did as he was told, without question. The speedometer needle rose quickly from the twenty-five to the fifty mark.

Martineau saw the tail lights of the Humber suddenly begin to dwindle. "No," he said to his own driver, as that young man put his foot down. "He may have spotted us. Let him go. We can't take any chances."

A moment later he said: "I think I know where he's going, anyway. I'll see if I can find out."

He called Headquarters, and asked for the position of the car which carried MacFarlane and Company. "It stopped at the junction of Dryshaw Lane and Hollins," he was told. "Another car came along Dryshaw, just a few seconds ago, and both cars have gone along one of those streets there, towards the Old Cemetery. Just at the moment we're out of touch with them."

"I want to speak to Superintendent Clay, or the Chief Constable," said Martineau.

It was the Chief himself who came on the air. "How are you doing, Martineau?"

"I'm almost certain that the objective is the Economic Society's head office, sir," was the reply. "The two suspect cars have dived into the little streets just there, within four hundred yards of it. I'm going there now. I think the men on duty there ought to be warned, and I suggest that the area be enclosed."

"It will be," said the Chief, "And I'll send you the first emergency squad to surround the main office building."

So at midnight the position was interesting. The head office of the society locally known as the Eco was almost certainly the target for tonight. The office building was surrounded on three sides by its own warehouses, acquired piecemeal as the great concern grew. On the fourth side was the Old Cemetery, thirty acres of small moss-grown tombstones and neglected graves, neglected because no one had been buried there within living memory. Lost among small streets somewhere near the Eco were the two suspect cars, with an unknown driver, Blundell, Bowie, Flint and MacFarlane in one, and an unknown driver with Connor in another, the driver probably being Carew and other passengers probably being Beadle, Novak and Hannah. Hannah had been lost to the police since he changed his lodgings after the incident of the detachable moustache. It was possible that Hannah had packed up and left town, but probable that he was in Connor's car. It was thought that there were ten gangsters in all, including the two drivers. This job was no diversion, it was the real thing.

The cemetery, which had never been a fashionable one, was regarded by some irreverent people as an eyesore, and by others as a waste of valuable real estate. The directors of the Economic had come to dislike its proximity, and they had figuratively shut their eyes to it by having all windows overlooking it bricked in. So on one long side of the office building, adjoining the cemetery, there was an unassailable windowless stretch of masonry five stories high. It was broken only in one place where there was a small yard, but even there the Eco had walled up all openings above ground level. They had also built a twenty-foot wall across the yard, leaving it totally enclosed, unused, and useless.

The police left the cemetery out of their calculations. They closed in on three sides. On the heels of the Plumber's men was Martineau with his picked detectives. On their way to surround the Eco building were the men of the first emergency squad. In the vicinity were various policemen on foot, and farther out, moving in from all directions to make a cordon, were thirty-two Area Patrol cars, fast Jaguars each with a crew of two men. It looked, as somebody at Headquarters remarked, as if the Granchester Gang had had it.

At the moment when Martineau ended his brief talk with the Chief, the first suspect car driven by Carew, and the second car, driven by the out-of-work taxi driver called Luke Whitehead, were arriving at a certain door of the Eco building. This was a door very much different from the resplendent front entrance which the general public saw. It was a plain board door with a big old-fashioned mortise lock, and it was locked but not barred because it was used by the watchmen on their rounds from building to building. Stanley Novak had seen the door and examined the lock. He now had a key in his pocket which would open it.

One of the uniformed policemen detailed to patrol outside the building happened to be standing within five feet of the door. That circumstance did not deter the Plumber. One car ran past the door and the other one stopped short of it, so that the P.C. was trapped.

The P.C. had not yet been informed of the likelihood of a raid upon the Eco, because it was only a few minutes since Martineau made his accurate guess about it. When the two cars stopped, the unfortunate officer wasted several vital seconds in wondering what it was all about. When masked men began to tumble out of the cars, his hand went to his whistle and the whistle went to his mouth. He blew one shrill blast upon it, then MacFarlane leapt upon him like a small-size tiger and struck a blow which drove the whistle into his throat. Bowie came up in support of the Scotsman, and on the other side came the Plumber. He coolly tipped off the policeman's helmet with one hand, and tapped him with the heavy pistol which he held in the other. The policeman collapsed. The Plumber stooped and yanked at the man's whistle chain. He snapped the thin, bright chain, and threw the whistle away.

The incident had caused practically no delay. The two cars were already moving away. Novak had gone straight to the door, and now it was open.

"Leave him there," the Plumber ordered. "Get inside."

Novak had already entered, and switched on lights. The other six trooped in after him. They were in a long room which seemed to be a storeroom, with a closed door at the other end. Novak relocked the outer door, put his key in his pocket, and crossed the room to the second door. The Plumber, coolly watching for every advantage, noticed that the outer door had bolts at top and bottom. He shot the bolts before he followed Novak.

The second door was locked. It had a glass panel and a cylinder lock. Delay, two seconds. Novak smashed the glass and reached through the opening to turn the latch.

Beyond the door was a corridor, which led to the back stairs. At the head of the stairs there was a solid, handsome door with a modern mortise lock. The door had a typical board-room look about it. "Quiet, now," the Plumber said.

Novak opened the door without noise in less than a minute. Beyond it there was a wide, lighted corridor, with executive offices on each side. At the end were big swing doors, obviously not locked. The seven masked men crept silently towards the doors, with the Plumber in the lead. At the door he listened for a moment, then, beckoning to the others, he charged into the general office.

In the general office, the policeman on guard had just received a phone call from Headquarters. As he put down the receiver he remarked: "There's going to be some excitement." Then he heard a slight creak as the big doors flew open, and he felt the draught. He saw his two companions, the watchmen, staring past him at the door. He turned, his right hand flying to his pistol holster. He saw six masked men, and six guns pointed in his direction.

Naturally the policeman had not expected the excitement to start quite so soon after the warning. His holster was buttoned and his gun was on safety. He realized that he did not have a chance. One of the masked men said "Reach," and the policeman reached.

Beadle the peterman had no interest in this Wild West caper. He went straight to the tall book safe. He started work with modelling clay, in preparation for pouring 'soup' into the lock. If his expression under the mask had been visible, it would have displayed contempt. The safe was hardly worthy of the attention of an expert like himself.

While Beadle worked, Flint, the warehouseman, took

strong cord from his pocket and tied up the policeman and the two watchmen. There was no need to gag the men. Very soon they would be able to make as much noise as they liked.

The Plumber put Bowie on guard at the swing door through which they had entered the room. He put MacFarlane outside another swing door, so that he could look down the wide stairway to the front entrance itself. He gave Blundell the easy task of guarding three bound men. Beadle still worked on the safe. Flint stood by with a sack which he had brought, ready to receive the money from the safe. Only paper money would be put in the sack. A few thousand pounds in silver and copper would be left behind.

With sentries set and the job going smoothly, the Plumber went with Novak to secure the retreat. He led the way down the main staircase to the front entrance. He looked at the front door, and found that it was locked, but not bolted. He beckoned to MacFarlane, and the little man came down the stairs two at a time.

"Shoot any man who tries to come in this way," the Plumber said, and MacFarlane nodded.

Under the main staircase there was an entrance to the cellar. The door was locked. The Plumber waited calmly and patiently while Novak opened it. In the cellar he found that the dim, dusty light bulbs were already burning. "There must be somebody down here," he said to Novak. The Pole marvelled at his apparent unconcern, and derived some comfort from it.

The Plumber paused to get his bearings, comparing his own position with the position of the front door. He took a piece of chalk from his pocket and made a mark on the dusty wall. "This way," he said.

The two men walked along a passage which had all the aspects of a tunnel. Then they turned and went past the open doorway of a boiler room, where a brawny man was shovelling coke. The man had his back to the doorway, and he did not see them.

They went on until they came to another corridor, and on one side of this corridor there were doorways at regular intervals. They were the doorways of empty rooms. "This is it," said the Plumber, and he made a mark on the wall.

The empty rooms were in darkness. The Plumber shone his torch into one after another and saw nothing but blank walls. "It's along here somewhere," he said, unflurried.

Eventually he shone his torch into a room with a window, just one window. The whole of it was below ground level, but it opened into a tiny area which was covered by a grating. It opened inwards. With gloved hands he jerked at the rusty handle and pulled it open. He climbed into the area and found that the grating was at shoulder height. With his head and his hands he pushed upward. The grating was stubborn, but he managed to move it without assistance from Novak. He lifted it aside and looked out into the enclosed yard which he had been seeking.

He flashed his torch around the yard and saw a ladder leaning against the wall. Leaning on the ladder was John Hannah.

"Good work, John," said the Plumber, just loud enough to be heard. "All goes well. Wait there."

He dropped down into the cellar. When he had gone, Hannah lit a cigarette. It was against orders, but he was in need of a smoke. He thought that his job, waiting and wondering, was the worst of all. And he had had to work alone. He had stolen a ladder in daylight, from a painter's yard. He had carried it into the cemetery and hidden it. After hiding the ladder he had watched for half an hour, to be sure that he had not been observed. Of course people had seen him in the street, carrying the ladder, but nobody had seemed to take much notice. Anybody who had noticed would keep quiet after learning how the ladder had been used. The Plumber had stopped folks from running to the police with every little thing they thought they knew.

At night Hannah had returned to the cemetery, picked up the ladder, got over the wall with it, reared it up on the inside, and waited. The waiting was awful. He smoked his cigarette hungrily. When he had done with it he nipped off the burning end and put the stub in his pocket. Absolutely no traces must be left, the Plumber had said.

The Plumber and Novak returned to the boiler room. The stoker was still working with his back to the door. The Plumber walked up behind him and hit him on the head with his pistol. The man fell on his face. The Plumber took cord from his pocket and threw it on the floor. He thought of everything. Flint had been told to bring cord; the Plumber had brought some in case Flint forgot.

"Tie him up," he said to Novak.

To save time he tied the man's ankles while Novak tied the hands. Then he led the way out of the cellar. He left Novak to guard the cellar-head and support MacFarlane in the event of an assault on the front door. There was just a possibility of that. A police whistle had been blown, and sometimes the police were very quick to gather after such an alarm.

When the Plumber was halfway up the main staircase he heard the detonation of Beadle's nitro-glycerine. He entered the main office and saw the Cockney peterman putting bundles of notes into a sack held by Flint. In two minutes or less, he calculated, the money would be in the bag. Nothing could go wrong now. With the plan itself nothing could have gone wrong, he told himself. It was some defect of the human element which he had feared: the carelessness, disobedience, and unpunctuality of irresponsible men. But once again discipline had been observed, and the men had acted perfectly in accordance with orders.

"All right, chum. There's plenty of time," he said calmly, as Beadle in his haste dropped a bundle of notes on the floor.

Somewhere there was a heavy thump. It was repeated, again and again. Beadle stopped work, and looked at the Plumber. Everybody looked at him, and mostly with alarm.

The Plumber was not perturbed. The thumping was obviously at the other end of the building. "Get on with it," he said to Beadle. "Don't leave any notes behind."

When all the notes were in the sack, Flint deftly tied the neck. Then Beadle took the sack and slung it on his shoulder. The distant thumping had stopped, and the Plumber became obsessed by a sense of urgency. But there was no sign of disquiet in the steady, sweeping gesture with which he commanded all his men to follow him out of the room. He ran down the main staircase, but it was a casual, unhurried sort of run. He knew that the slightest sign of panic in himself would cause a loss of self-possession in the others.

Before he reached the bottom of the stairs there was a tremendous thump on the front door. That was the police, all right, he decided. And they would soon burst the door.

"You know the way," he said to Novak, and he stood while his men trooped down into the cellar: Novak, Beadle, Blundell, Bowie, Flint and MacFarlane. There was another assault upon the door, and a loud, ominous crack. The Plumber fled into the cellar, and closed the door behind him. There was no key in the cellar door, and it had no bolt. But, he reflected, it would be a few minutes before the police discovered which way he had gone.

He had intended to delay the police further by rubbing out his own chalk arrows, but now he had no time for that. He hurried after his men, and caught up with them. While he waited for the last of them to climb out of the cellar into the enclosed yard he looked at his watch. Not bad, he decided. The job had taken exactly eleven minutes, from entering the building and leaving it.

CHAPTER FIFTEEN

WHEN the Plumber and his men arrived at the rear door of the Eco office building, the constable on duty at the front heard the two cars. He heard them stop, and he heard the banging of the car doors. Amid the banging of doors he heard the single brief blast of a police whistle. Then he heard the cars move away.

There had not yet been time to inform this officer of the impending raid, and when he heard the cars his first idea was it was a visit of inspection. The Chief and a few more of the top brass, he thought, going the rounds. The brief alarm upon the whistle did not immediately dispel the idea. A police rallying call was a good deal longer and louder than that. Old George acting a bit windy, the P.C. thought. Starting to blow his whistle before he knew what it was all about.

But the cars were driven away at once, having stopped only long enough for men to alight. And the P.C. remembered that old George was not a windy type at all. So there might be something wrong. Something wrong? And quarter of a million pounds upstairs there? The P.C. took out his Enfield ·45. He went to see what was wrong.

He found his mate lying on the ground, snoring stertorously. He propped him against the side of the building and went to the rear door. It was secure, and unmarked. He was pondering about that when a watchman crossed the street from another of the Eco buildings. "Open me that door," he said to the watchman.

The watchman put his key in the lock, and turned it. "It won't open," he said.

"Barred on the inside," said the P.C., and he set off to run to the nearest police telephone.

He ran into Martineau, who was getting out of a car round the first corner. "All right, what is it?" came the crisp question.

The P.C. told his story. "I think it must be a duplicate key job, sir," he concluded.

"How long since you heard the whistle?" the inspector asked.

"Not more than two minutes ago, sir."

Martineau nodded. The man was human. Call it three minutes. "Blow your whistle, loud and long," he said.

The Plumber did not hear that whistle, because he had just gone into the cellar with Novak. But up in the main office his men heard it. Beadle went on with his work. The others looked at each other, their masks hiding consternation. But they stood their ground. The Plumber had told them not to worry if the police surrounded the building.

Outside, men and cars were arriving, and Martineau spent several minutes in making sure that the building *was* surrounded. "Is there any way out on the cemetery side?" he asked the watchman, and the man replied: "No way out."

Another inspector arrived, and Martineau handed over the command of the cordon. "It might be a good idea to send some men into the cemetery, just in case," he advised. "I'm going to try and get into this place."

He went to the rear door, and found Devery there. "We can't bust that without a battering ram," the sergeant said. After trying the door, Martineau agreed. He called to the watchman: "How can we get in?"

"I only have a key for that one," the watchman replied.

"Then we'll have to break in. Which door will be easiest?"

"The main entrance, I should think. It's a double-leaf door, and one side isn't barred."

Martineau, Devery, and their following of half a dozen detectives hurried round to the front door. While they were still on their way, they heard a muffled exploson. "They're in, all right," said Martineau. "There goes the safe."

The front door was handsome, a fine craftsman's job. It was so wide that four men could put their shoulders against the half of it which carried the lock. The lock was strong, but repeated assaults finally burst open the door. The idea of shooting into the lock did not occur to any man there. None of them was accustomed to having a gun in his possession.

They went in with a rush, and saw the empty front hall and the empty staircase. Upstairs there was a hullaballoo. Men were shouting for help. Somehow that seemed wrong to Martineau, but he had no time to ponder about it.

Had he but known which way to go, he was then only half a minute behind the Plumber, who was hurrying through the cellar at that moment.

He ran up the stairs, and entered the main office. The tumult and the shouting died. "Which way did they go?" he asked the trussed policeman.

"The way you came in. I heard them running down the stairs."

"You're sure of that?"

"I'm certain. They all had rubber shoes, but I heard 'em all right."

Martineau left him, and ran back down the stairs. At the foot he met the watchman, who had discovered that the cellar door was not locked.

"Bill Sparks locked himself in when he went down there," the man said. "Special precaution."

"Is there any other way out of the cellar?"

"Not as I know of. Only the chutes."

"Take me to Bill Sparks."

They went into the cellar. Martineau had been delayed about a minute, while the Plumber had been in full retreat. There was now nearly two minutes' difference between pursuers and pursued.

In the boiler room they found Bill Sparks, with a bruised and bloody face. He was sitting up and trying to wriggle out of his bonds. The watchman cut him loose while Martineau talked to him.

"Is there any way out of this cellar on the cemetery side?" demanded the inspector, who had become afflicted by a dreadful suspicion.

"There's a window, but nobody could get out that way," Sparks replied.

"Why?"

"It leads into a closed yard. There's a twenty-foot wall."

"Oh, my God!" said Martineau brokenly. So that was why the Plumber had sent his transport away. The cars would be waiting for him in the cemetery. It could be so. Or it could be some sort of trick to draw the pursuit.

"Did you see anybody at all?" he asked Sparks.

"I saw a crowd of 'em, seven or eight. They all had black cloths over their faces. They went past that opening about five minutes ago, and one of 'em had a sack on his back."

"Going towards the cellar window?"

"Going that way, yes."

That settled it. Martineau turned to a detective. "Get to a phone," he said. "Get Headquarters. Tell them the Plumber may be escaping through the Old Cemetery. He probably has transport in the cemetery. In my name ask for the second emergency squad to cordon the cemetery. And ask for a strong mobile cordon a long way farther out. Just short of Shirwell and Broadshaw, I'd say. Then get some men and search, first this cellar, then the whole building."

Then Martineau turned to the stoker, who seemed to know more about the place than the watchman. "If there's a ladder on the premises," he said, "I want it."

"We do have a ladder," the stoker replied. "But I don't know if it's a twenty-footer."

The man looked sick, and he was unsteady on his feet, so two detectives went with him to get the ladder. Martineau went in search of the window, and found it. In the yard, Devery pointed to the marks where the iron-tipped ends of Hannah's ladder had pressed into the accumulated dirt. Unfortunately, the dirt was not soft enough to show clear footmarks.

They waited. The men were silent, sensing Martineau's mood. The inspector was beginning to feel very bitter. And apprehensive. It looked as if the Plumber had outwitted him. At any time during the evening he could have laid his hands on five or six of the Plumber's men, and he had gone and let them commit the biggest robbery which had ever been perpetrated in Granchester.

The ladder was brought, and pushed through the window. It was several feet short of the top of the wall, but it enabled the policemen to scramble over and take a long drop into a bed of willow herb on the other side. One detective sprained his ankle, but he did not mention his injury until the chase had ended.

The party, seven men in all, spread out in a long line and made their way across the cemetery. Martineau guessed that the Plumber would now be about ten minutes ahead of him. If the Plumber had motor transport waiting, that ten minutes would be altogether decisive: the man would have got clean away. The thought was unbearable, and Martineau put it from him. He called to his men: "Press on!"

There was no question of secrecy now. As the men moved in line their strong flashlights illuminated the alleys between the gravestones. It was a hurried and superficial search, but sufficient to show that no gang of thieves was hiding in the

146

cemetery. One man called out: "Here's their ladder!" but Martineau replied: "Keep going!"

* * * * *

When they parted from their accomplices at the back door of the Economic office buildings, the Plumber's drivers, Carew and Whitehead, did not move away together. They started to drive out of the warehouse district by slightly divergent routes, but with the same destination. Each of them had been instructed to circle widely and approach the Old Cemetery unobserved from the other side. From the quiet side, as the Plumber had phrased it.

Their job should have been easy, and they had expected it to be easy. They should have had ample time to get out of the danger zone and, probably, reach the rendezvous. The shrill blast of a policeman's whistle initially disturbed their composure, but when they had gone some distance without seeing any sign of police activity their confidence returned. Then, at about the same time but in different places, they each encountered units of the mobile cordon which was forming.

Whitehead gave the police no trouble at all. He was neither rash, brave nor belligerent. Greed alone made him a criminal. Greed was his strength, and his weakness was a touching faith in his own ability to deceive. He was a man who always thought he could get away with it, whatever it was.

He calculated that if anything went wrong with this Eco job, then he at least would be in the clear. He was only a driver. He had no gun, and no mask. He had nothing in his pockets by which he could be identified and, by great good fortune, the owner of the car he drove was one of those men who kept both driving licence and certificate of insurance in the door pocket. There were no incriminating fingerprints on the car, and the car was not 'hot'.

This last advantage was due to the Plumber's foresight. He would never permit the use of a hot car on a job of this sort. So he had himself indicated which car should be used.

It was the property of a wholesale fish merchant who went to bed early because he had to get up early. The fish merchant was sound asleep, his garage had been opened by one of Novak's keys, and it had been left open so that any policeman who saw it would assume that the owner was still out somewhere with his car.

Whitehead had looked at the driving licence, and he knew the wealthy fish merchant's name and address by heart. What he did *not* know was that the police were already barring his way, and that on this night of nights they were not going to let any man pass without an interrogation thorough enough to gain him entry to the U.S.A., or the U.S.S.R., or Heaven, or Hell. So when he was stopped he did not try to run, he tried to bluff his way out.

The car which caused him to stop pulled in across his front, and a scowling young giant jumped out and came running to him—of all things!—gun in hand. The sight of the gun shook Whitehead: he had never before seen a policeman with a gun. He realized that it was indeed high time that the Plumber's gang went out of business. Luke Whitehead, he decided, was going out of it right now, as soon as he had got away from this flatfoot.

"What seems to be the matter, officer?" he asked mildly, speaking, as he thought, in the way which the owner of such a car would speak.

The policeman peered into his face. "I seem to know your clock," he said. "This your own car?"

"It is. Do you wish to see my licence?"

Whitehead reached for the door pocket, and the gun came up to within six inches of his head. "Take your hand out of there empty," the policeman growled. "I'll get the licence."

He did not get the licence. The second policeman had arrived. He was a stout man, older than his mate by twenty years.

"Hallo, Luke," he said jovially. He gazed at the car as if in admiration. "Travelling rolls-roycey, aren't you? Where did you huff this?"

"You're mistaken, officer," said Whitehead with dignity. "I did not, er, huff it."

"We won't argue about it, Lukie boy," the stout man replied. "You know the drill. Anything you say will be taken down in writing and all that bull. See if he has a gun, Dave, and then you can get in with him and let him drive you to H.Q. I'll tag on behind."

*   *   *   *   *

The case of Motor Patrol *versus* Nigel Carew was altogether more spectacular. Carew was an escaped convict who could not stand the scrutiny of any police officer. He was armed, and if necessary he would kill in order to get away.

He was driving steadily along his prearranged route when a big car overtook him and decreased speed a few yards ahead of him. The 'Stop-Police' sign was switched on.

Carew stopped, and put his car into reverse gear. When the police car had stopped, and a policeman was out in the road and coming towards him, he accelerated rearward. He drove skilfully, as fast as the car would go in reverse gear. Before the policeman had regained his own car, Carew had backed until he could turn along a side street. He sped away, still going in the right direction but by a shorter route.

The police car pursued, with its radio giving out notice of locality, direction and speed. Two more police cars closed in, accurately guessing where Carew would emerge from a labyrinth of small streets. One of them stopped right across the end of the outlet street as Carew came racing along it. He swerved on to the sidewalk and drove between a lamp post and the wall. There was not quite enough room for the big Humber, but Carew was such an excellent driver that he touched with both sides of the car as he scraped through. He went on, but a slight change in the quality of the car's steering warned him that he had done more than scrape the paint. Actually, one front wing had been pushed in so that it was scraping on the wall of the tyre and cutting away a shaving of rubber with every turn of the wheel.

However, the car would still 'motor', and Carew felt that it would now be an exceptional police driver who could keep him in sight. But he guessed that he was in a trap. The two police cars had been much too near to each other to be on an ordinary routine prowl. Therefore, he thought, other police cars would be in the vicinity. Absent-mindedly he began to whistle a little tune. Two cars behind him, and how many in front? How much running about would he have to do before he could afford to get out and have a look at that bent wing?

He came to a place where the road ran like a canyon between long, high factories. There was no turning here for half a mile, and at the other end was the bright, red gleam of a watchman's brazier. Road work in progress apparently, but there would be a way through. He went on. In his driving mirror the headlights of a following car were reflected. The car seemed to be gaining on him just a little. He said to himself that those police Jags certainly could motor.

As he drew nearer to the glowing brazier he saw the dim red gleam of danger lamps, and they indicated that the open part of the road was on the right-hand side. He discerned the outline of the watchman's hut, not much bigger than a sentry box. Then, to the right of the brazier he saw the lights of a car. It was coming towards him through the narrow lane left by the roadmenders.

He swore, but not ill-humouredly because he was never really out of temper when he was driving. He decreased speed, estimating that the oncoming car would be barely clear of the narrow place when he reached it. Then the car stopped, blocking the way, and he knew that it was yet another police car.

Carew had about three seconds in which to make up his mind. He did not need so many. 'Trials stuff,' he muttered. If he could get through here he would gain hundreds of yards and get clear of the cordon. There was just room enough for him to knock the brazier sideways and get through to the left of the police car. He would be in the excavation, which was probably only eight or nine inches deep if it was a re-surfacing job. He would skittle lamps and rope-posts, and he might get entangled. That was a chance he had to take. He thought he could get through.

He held his speed until the last fraction of a second. Then he slowed, aiming to pass as near to the stationary car as he could. He became aware of a tall figure wearing the peaked cap of the motor patrol. This person was standing right in his way between the car and the brazier, waving a danger lamp. 'If you don't skip aside, chum, you've had it,' was the thought in his mind. That was the moment when the turned edge of the wing finished its work on the left front tyre. The tyre burst.

The car lurched. It charged straight at the watchman's box, and Carew could see the watchman, a little old man with only one arm, sitting staring at him in helpless terror. But Carew had been born and raised a gentleman, and with no time for second thoughts he instinctively acted like one. He held the car with a skill which was also instinctive, and succeeded in steering away from the man in the box. He hit the iron basket of bright pink glowing coke with the middle of his front fender.

A shower of fire erupted from the brazier. It went flying into the shallow excavation, and the car followed it with a clutter of ropes, iron posts, and danger lamps. The car hit it again, and crumpled and overrode it, so that it was dragged along somewhere underneath, hooked by a leg to some part of the chassis.

Now the car was in a state which could be called unmanageable, but somehow Carew managed it. There was a heap of sand facing him, and it was handily situated near the right hand edge of the excavation. He used the sand to get up and out on to the road. In doing so he crushed the remains of the brazier against the abrupt concrete rim of the excavation. Some broken part of it pierced the petrol tank. Fuel ran out of the hole, into the excavation, where burning cinders were scattered around. Fire followed the car and overtook it. Fire enveloped the rear of it. In his driving mirror, Carew saw red flame. He scrambled out of the car,

Two men pursued him. The policemen from the car, obviously. One of them shouted "Stop!" Carew sprinted.

But one of the policemen was a better runner than Carew, He gained. Carew took his gun from his pocket and thumbed the safety catch. He stopped, turned, and fired. He saw the leading policeman stumble, and he ran on.

The second policeman followed, and he also began to overtake Carew. "Stop, you mad fool!" he called, and fired his service revolver. It was only a warning shot, because in Britain armed policemen shoot only to protect themselves or others, and not to bring down fleeing criminals.

Carew did not know that. He expected a bullet in his back. He took the first turning, the first opening he could see. He found himself, not in a side street, but in a big factory yard. And it was a tidy, empty yard. There was nothing to give him cover. There was not even the darkness of a loading bay to give him an advantage.

Around the yard there were big shutter doors and smaller doors. A small door in the far corner showed a faint reflective gleam, as if it had a glass panel. Carew made for it. 'If I can get inside the factory,' he thought, 'I can elude this clod-hopper.'

He reached the door. It had a glass panel and a mortise lock. He broke the glass with his pistol. The policeman, who had taken the corner with caution, came pounding across the yard towards him.

Carew put his hand through the opening he had made, feeling for the key on the inner side of the door. There was no key. He turned in the doorway and fired at the oncoming policeman, and missed. The policeman returned his fire. Like most policemen, he had seen military service. And as it happened, most of his service had been in a Royal Marine commando. He was well-trained in the use of hand guns, and according to his training he aimed instinctively and accurately at the heart. The big service revolver roared twice, and Nigel Carew, who might have had an honourable and brilliant career, died like a rat in a corner.

CHAPTER SIXTEEN

WHEN the Plumber reached the empty, open square in the centre of the Old Cemetery he realized that some part of his foolproof plan had gone wrong. Two cars with two drivers should have been waiting for him there. They had had plenty of time, but they had not arrived. Therefore they would not be coming. Therefore they had been captured or chased away by the police. The police had been suspiciously close upon his heels tonight, he reflected. It looked as if they had had some sort of prior knowledge of the raid. The Plumber was disturbed by that conclusion, but like a good commander he maintained an air of calm.

"It looks as if we're on foot, men," he observed. "But don't let it bother you. We'll get through all right. We'll stick together for the time being, and maybe we'll be able to find some sort of transport."

Then Blundell showed that in spite of nervous strain he was not entirely bereft of intelligence. "We can cut straight through to York Road from the cemetery gate," he said. "There's an all-night transport café with a parking ground. We should find something there."

"A good idea, Owen," the Plumber approved. "If you know the way, lead on. We need not run, but we'll walk fast."

They went on, making good time down the main drive of the cemetery. They were very much on the alert as they approached the gate, but they met no policemen. "We're still ahead of them," said the Plumber. "I doubt if they'll find us now."

Eight men walking all together along deserted midnight streets cannot easily affect to be casual. The Plumber thought about that and decided that masks would still be worn, because anonymity was still a primary consideration. He sent Blundell and Bowie ahead, walking one on each side of the narrow way which Blundell chose. He followed some twenty yards behind, walking with Beadle, MacFarlane, and Novak. He put Flint and Hannah in a rearguard position, twenty yards farther back still, an interval which those two nerve-worn men quickly reduced to about five yards. The Plumber was aware of the encroachment, but he pretended not to notice. 'Don't worry the men,' he warned himself. 'Keep them in good heart.'

When Martineau reached the cemetery gate the Plumber was half a mile away. He found the second emergency squad newly arrived, and the Plumber gone, lost to him in a labyrinth of deserted streets among mills and warehouses.

"They're away," he said to Devery in a heart-broken voice. "They've got clean away."

Then he received the news that the enemy's transport had been put out of action. He heard of Whitehead's arrest and Carew's death.

"They're on foot, then," he said with renewed hope. "They're on foot until they can get hold of a vehicle, at any rate."

He considered the position from where he stood: the streets which fanned away from the cemetery gate, and where they led. From a police car which had arrived he reported the situation to Headquarters, and made suggestions as to what should be done. The men of the second emergency squad could remain where they were until the Plumber had been located. They could serve the double purpose of surrounding the cemetery and forming the base line of the wide cordon which was forming. The cars which were still in the vicinity of the Economic buildings could race round and strengthen the new cordon. "Spread your net plenty wide enough," he advised. "Our clients must be ten or fifteen minutes ahead of me. They could be a mile away right now."

The Chief Constable had left Headquarters to go to the scene of action, and Superintendent Clay was in charge of Headquarters. He promised full co-operation. "I think we've got 'em now," he said confidently. "We swung wide enough at the start and they can't have got away. Somebody will spot 'em any minute now."

Martineau got out of the car and went to Devery. "It looks as if we shall have to stay here until there's some news," he said. "We seem to have them sewed up."

The idea of being at the wrong side of the cordon when the Plumber tried to break out did not appeal to Devery. "How about getting a car and going forward?" he suggested. "They might try to cross York Road. We can see half a mile either way along there."

"We'll try it," was the answer. They went to the car, and a young detective called Derbyshire followed them hopefully. He waited anxiously while the two senior officers got into the car, and when Martineau nodded to him he joined them with alacrity.

"No lights," said Martineau to the uniformed driver. "Drive through to York Road. Nice and steady."

The driver said "Yessir," and started the car, and in a few minutes he was nosing carefully out into a wide, straight arterial road. The long vista of the road was ablaze with yellow sodium lamps, and scattered neon signs added colour to the glare.

"Pull up," ordered Martineau. "We'll sit still for a couple of minutes and see what's moving."

The men lowered the car windows and stared along the bright, deserted road. Martineau looked at the lighted sign of the Belmont Transport Café two hundred yards away. He considered the possibilities of the place. Half a score of commercial vehicles were standing on the parking ground there: unattended vehicles whose drivers were having a cup of coffee or a meal.

He was still looking thoughtfully at the café when a carrier's van, a three-tonner by the look of it, pulled out of the parking ground and burbled away along the road. As it did so there was a shout. It was a doubtful sort of shout, as if some driver had called out in farewell to another driver of whose identity he was not certain.

"Just tool along towards the café, will you?" Martineau said to his driver.

Still watching, he saw a man appear from behind a row of parked lorries and enter the café. Then, as the car drew near, another man ran out of the café. He sprinted across the parking ground and into the road. He stared after the retreating van, then looked wildly about him and saw the police car.

"Somebody's just pinched my bloody van!" he bawled.

The police driver called across to him. "What make and number?"

"It's a Bedford. A double Z eight eight seven," was the excited reply. "It has 'Vale Transport' painted on the side."

"Right. Stay at the café. We'll contact you later."

155

As the car pursued the van, Martineau passed on the details to Clay at Headquarters. "Maybe we're on the Plumber's tail, or maybe it isn't the Plumber at all," he ended cautiously.

Moving at high speed, the police car was drawing near to the van. "Put your lights on and close up," said Martineau. "They're bound to see us in this light."

As the car drew nearer, its occupants could see that the van was of a common carrier's type. It had a high shed, and an open back with a raised tailboard instead of van doors. Nearer still, faces appeared above the tailboard, and shots were fired. A starred hole appeared in the windscreen of the car.

"Drop back a bit and follow from a distance," said Martineau. "We had no instructions to get killed. I saw five faces behind that tailboard. With two men in the cab, or maybe three, that makes seven or eight in all. It's the gang all right, and they're sticking together."

He spoke to Clay again. "It's the Plumber all right, and most of his gang," he said. "They took a shot at us without even bothering to make sure we were bobbies. We're following them down York Road into town. We're passing the York Road Odeon, if you want our exact location."

"So now we know," came Clay's reply. "We've got him. Report his position every two minutes, and I'll make a net he can't possibly get out of."

Martineau left the radio at 'receive'. "It's in the bag," he said.

But, net or no net, he made a private resolve to keep in touch with the van at all costs. He was not going to allow the Plumber's gang to abandon it and scatter.

* * * * *

In the van, the Plumber was driving. Beside him sat Blundell, who was also a capable driver. Beside Blundell sat Beadle, with a sackful of currency at his feet. In the rear of the van were Bowie, Flint, Hannah, MacFarlane and Novak. At the Plumber's suggestion Blundell had knocked the glass out of the little window at the back of the cab, so that instructions and information could be freely passed from front to rear.

Thus the Plumber was quickly told that a car was overtaking the van. "Well, you've got guns, haven't you?" he replied, still maintaining his pose of imperturbability.

Shots were fired, and then somebody called: "They've dropped back, but they're still after us. They're coppers, all right."

"Never mind," the Plumber answered cheerfully. "Just make them keep their distance. We'll see the cash safely delivered, and then I'm going to take you all home and put you to bed."

Two or three of the men laughed, and the Plumber smiled grimly in the darkness of the cab. He knew that the business of getting away from the police was not going to be any sort of laughing matter. This part of the job was not at all as he had planned. 'Maybe they'll weep before the night's out,' he thought.

He drove straight into town, believing that the police would be less likely to make a correct interpretation of his movements if their own arrangements made him turn aside. He approached the junction of York Road and Bishopsgate, and saw cars barring the way.

"Road block," said Beadle stolidly. His phlegmatic manner concealed a deep uneasiness. So far as he knew nobody had been shot, yet. Yet. The way the job had turned out it looked as if there were going to be bloodshed aplenty.

On the right of the road near to the junction were several streets which led into Darktown, which was just the place where the Plumber wanted to be. He turned away from the main road just as if he had been compelled to do so by the road block, and soon he was turning this way and that among the little, miserable streets of Darktown as if he were concerned only with getting away from the car which followed him. "Make those bobbies keep their distance," he warned his men.

Several times he drove along a street and then doubled back along the next parallel street, so that for as much as ten seconds at a time he was out of sight of the police driver.

He did this so that the police driver would become used to the manœuvre, and so that the police would not be able to guess just where an important fugitive had alighted.

The important fugitive was Beadle, the man with the money. Beadle could be trusted not to abscond with the money. In the first place he was not the sort of man to abscond, and in the second place he knew that if he did abscond at least three members of the gang would never cease to hunt for him until they had found him and killed him. The three men were the Plumber, Hannah, and MacFarlane. Beadle would not abscond.

Eventually the Plumber doubled back along the street where the Golden Fleece Inn stood. The police car was out of sight. Near the dark, shabby little pub the van slowed. Beadle opened the door beside him, and got out on to the step. He reached back for the sack of money and hauled it out. Then he jumped, and vanished like a shadow into the opening at the side of the tavern. When he had gone, Blundell caught the swinging door and held it an inch or two open. He held it thus for some time. When he eventually slammed it, the van was a long way from the tavern.

With the sack of money, Beadle went to the back door of the Golden Fleece. He did not knock, but stood in a sweat of anxiety until it was silently opened. The landlord reached for the sack, but Beadle pushed him back and stepped inside.

"Shut the door and bar it," he whispered hoarsely.

"But I thought——"

"Shut the perishing door! There's been a change of plans. I'm staying here till morning. I wouldn't go out again tonight if you was to give me the Crown Jewels. The flaming town is alive with coppers."

"It was a van. What happened to the cars?"

"We lost 'em. I guess the bogies got 'em. It's been a hell of a do. But we're all right so far, I think."

"But I can't let you stay here. I——"

In the total darkness behind the door Beadle's fierce whisper rustled and echoed. "You just try and put me out! There's nearly a quarter of a million quid here, and I'm staying with it. You just find me somewhere to lay down, and your job's done. Show us a ha'porth of guts, man! You'll wake up in the morning and find yourself rich."

Meanwhile, in the cab of the van, the Plumber was speaking in a good-humoured tone to Blundell.

"We're edging out towards Shirwell now," he said. "Make up your mind where you want to get off."

"The streets in Shirwell are different. They're more sort of open," Blundell objected.

"True; too true. But they also offer more cover. You'll have to drop off as we go round a corner, and then get down behind one of those little garden walls."

Blundell pondered.

"It'll have to be the school, then," he said. "I'll show you the way when we get into Shirwell."

As he considered it, the big new secondary school was ideal for his purpose. There was a low front wall and a big school yard, and behind the school buildings were wide playing fields. He could cross the yard and the playing fields, and be far from street lights and patrolling policemen. And when he crossed the fields he would be nearly home.

For the Plumber there was the problem of getting into Shirwell. It was all right driving round and round the little streets of Darktown, but he would have to cross a main road to get out of it.

"The vultures are gathering while we're playing hide and seek with this chap behind," he said. "Apply your great mind to the problem. How are we going to get across Dock Road?"

"You mean we'll be blocked in?" asked Blundell, startled.

"I shall be very surprised if we aren't. You've lived all your life around these parts. Can you find us a way out?"

"A way out into Dock Road," Blundell murmured thoughtfully, and then he was silent. In a little while he said: "We can get out if we can knock a couple of gates down."

"What sort of gates?"

"Wooden gates. Brown's, the builder's merchant's. There's a yard full of door-stones and drainpipes and stuff. The back gate is in Alabama Street and the front gate is in Dock Road, and it's a straight drive through the yard."

"Good boy," said the Plumber. "We'll do the job in reverse, then we won't damage the van."

He drove straight to Dock Road then, and when he came within sight of it he saw that the way was blocked by two police cars. "What now?" he asked.

"Keep going," said Blundell. "Take the last turning on the right, just before you come to the road block."

The Plumber took the turning as directed, and drove along a back street which ran parallel to Dock Road. Martineau's car followed him.

Every two hundred yards or so the back street crossed a street which joined Dock Road, and at every junction the Plumber saw one or two police cars. Also, another police car was keeping pace with him along Dock Road, ready to act as a reinforcement at any place where he might try to break out. "All right. We'll fox you, my fine fellow," he muttered.

"Here it is," said Blundell. "On the left."

"I see it," said the Plumber. He called: "You men in the back! Sit on the floor and keep away from the tailboard!"

The Plumber drove a yard or two past the gate, turned right as if were going to run into a house end, and braked suddenly. He put the van into reverse gear and, turning the wheel to get a full lock, he backed into the gate. The gate flew open and the van was not halted for even a fraction of a second. Leaning out of the cab window and looking rearward, the Plumber reversed across the yard with one hand on the wheel. He maintained a good speed, because he knew that the second gate would not merely have to be pushed open. To make it open outward it would have to be torn from its hinges and broken down.

He saw the gateposts silhouetted against the lights of Dock Road. He steered to miss the gatepost on his side, and the van hit the gate with great force. There was a rending, crackling sound, and a crash. The gate was broken and knocked out of the way, and the van rolled out into Dock Road. As it did so, Martineau's car entered the yard through the other gateway.

In the road the Plumber straightened out and engaged a forward gear. The car which had been running parallel to his course was ahead of him, and its driver was hastily reversing to turn round in the road. The Plumber took the nearest side street, and rumbled away towards Shirwell.

*　　*　　*　　*　　*

As his car continued to follow the van, Martineau informed Headquarters that the Plumber had broken through the inner ring of the cordon. When he had done, he said to Devery: "Have you got the idea yet?"

"I think so," said Devery. "This game of follow-my-leader isn't just a matter of trying to shake us off. Why did our friend go to all that trouble to get across Dock Road? Because he's taking Blundell home."

"And then he'll try and take Flint home. And I have a sneaking suspicion that he dropped somebody in Darktown. He did a lot of twisting and turning and then suddenly made a bee-line for Dock Road."

"So what do we do about it?"

"Nothing. Blundell and Flint can go home in peace, and the observers will note times of arrival. They can be picked up later. There'll still be Connor, Bowie, Beadle and MacFarlane in the van, and those are the boys we want. In a little while those lads are going to try to get back into town, to creep into their holes. That's when the fun will really start."

*　　*　　*　　*　　*

Before the van got as far as Shirwell, Bernard Flint scrambled over the boxes and cartons with which it was half-loaded, and spoke to the Plumber.

"I'm right anywhere about here," he said. "Me an' Stanley can drop off an' get along back streets an' across the allotments to Churlham. There'll be no cops the way I'll go."

"Right, Barney," was the cheery answer. "I'll go slow when I've turned the next corner, and you can take your chance."

It was customary for Novak to go home with Flint, because Novak lived eight miles away, in Boyton. Flint would let him out of the house before the children were awake, and he would travel home safely enough in the company of workers who started their jobs in the Boyton cotton mills at seven o'clock.

Flint and Novak chose a suitable moment and climbed over the tailboard. They took cover behind a tiny privet hedge as the police car went by. Novak thought that they had been observed, but Flint said: "Well, they kept going. Come on, let's get home before they get busy with their wireless."

Three minutes later Blundell opened the door of the cab and moved out on to the step of the van. He was the youngest and the most agile of the Plumber's men. As the van turned the corner near the school he leaped lightly to the ground and ran to the schoolyard wall. He vaulted over it and dropped flat on the other side. He lay there panting in concealment like a terrified animal. He did not move until the sound of the van and its attendant car had died away.

"Four men safely delivered," the Plumber called cheerily to the men in the back of the van. "Now we've got to get into town."

"Now the fireworks start," MacFarlane replied. It was a simple statement of fact.

The Plumber nodded to himself. He had been trying to think constructively about the business of getting back to town. Hannah, Bowie, MacFarlane and himself were all middle-of-town residents. They lived in different circumstances to be sure, but all within the same half-mile square. And they had to get home. There was no point in heading out into the suburbs and then trying to sneak back separately in daylight. It couldn't be done; not with this damned police car hanging on to their tail. They had to get home, and in darkness. Darkness was their element: the night was a friend.

He thought about the enemy. The police, God rot them. They would have the fugitive van nicely pinpointed on their big table map, and they would be making their arrangements according to its position. He knew how they worked: he had fooled them often enough. But tonight, he thought, they had him. Or at least, they had the van. Well, they could have the van.

"Any suggestions about getting home?" he asked.

Apparently no one had any suggestions, so he went on: "They'll have us surrounded, you know. They'll want us to kill ourselves by running into a road block." Then he added, with mild humour which was wasted upon his companions: "We don't want to do that."

There was still no comment, so he continued: "We don't want to get downhearted. We've not been unsuccessful, so far. We've dumped the boodle, and it's safe. Every man will get his share. And the police haven't caught anybody yet."

Bowie asked: "What about Whitehead and Carew?"

The Plumber detected a note of stupid resentment in the question. Bowie! This was a hell of a time to make trouble.

"We don't know, do we?" he answered crisply. "And no matter what has happened to them, they won't talk. They'll try to keep clear of this job, and not talk themselves into it."

"Yeh, that's right," growled Hannah. A dour man, but the most loyal of them all.

The Plumber did not say anything more for a while. He was approaching a main street. It appeared to be unguarded. He rolled across it, and went on, travelling at a right angle to his destination. He was determined to go as far as he could in this direction, because he wanted to get into Boyton Road. Along Boyton Road he would have a clear run into his own part of the town, provided that nobody stopped him. He went on and on, cutting across that part of the city, and the police car followed him faithfully. He reflected that the police net was wide indeed. He did not know that Superintendent Clay had made an accurate guess about the last part of his journey. Clay was giving him access to Boyton Road. Clay wanted him in Boyton Road.

Eventually the Plumber gave his final instructions: "I'm going to crash through as far as I can, without getting damaged too much. When you hear me shout, sit down and hang on to something. When we're stopped, it'll be every man for himself. Is that clear?"

Hannah and MacFarlane said that they understood. Bowie did not answer.

"Right," said the Plumber. "We're coming to Boyton Road now."

Half a minute later he emerged into the brilliantly lighted main road. It was the road from Granchester to Boyton, and to Huddersfield, Halifax, Bradford, Leeds; Hull, Middlesbrough, Sunderland, Newcastle. Thereabouts it was straight for several miles. The only vehicles in sight were three huge lorries which were travelling in convoy towards Boyton. 'If the police decide to block the road with some of those things,' the Plumber mused, 'we might as well give up.'

He turned towards the centre of the city, and drove the van as hard as it would go. Almost at once an area patrol car appeared and came surging up behind him, its warning bell making a devil's din in the quiet, cool night. Behind the A. P. car, Martineau's car emerged into the main road and followed.

MacFarlane and Hannah fired at the A. P. car, and it dropped back. MacFarlane hooded his torch and looked at the van's load. He began to ease the strain of inactivity by dropping boxes and parcels into the path of the pursuing cars. The police drivers avoided the objects skilfully.

Hannah reloaded his gun, and he told his companions to do the same. "We've got to be ready for aught," he said.

Far ahead of him at a crossroads, the Plumber saw two cars appear. They stopped, barring the way. He considered their position in relation to the crossing. He had to get past them somehow. It was no use turning aside now. If he did, the cars in front and the cars behind would run parallel to his course and block him in completely among little streets. This, he decided, was the showdown. The cat wasn't playing with the mouse any more.

He reduced his speed as he drew near to the two cars. Their crews had left them, and were standing on the sidewalks. There was no way between the cars. On the near side the sidewalk was blocked by a lamp post. On the offside there was room to get by if the van was strong enough to nudge the front end of a police car about a foot to one side.

164

That collision could put the van out of action, but the risk had to be taken. The van mounted the kerb at a moderate speed, and the Plumber shouted to his companions: "Hold tight!" The policemen at the corner stood their ground until the last moment, then they jumped aside. The Plumber took no notice of them. They had guns in their hands, but he knew that they would not fire unless they were fired upon.

He got through all right, with serious but not crippling damage. As the van gathered speed after the collision, a policeman jumped and seized the tailboard, with the intention of scrambling aboard. Hannah and Bowie hammered his fingers with their guns, and he had to let go. He never knew how lucky he was. They could have blown his head off.

The Plumber went on his way, and the pursuing police cars came through the opening he had made. The road was clear for half a mile. "We're getting near home!" he cried jubilantly.

Far ahead, at the next crossroads, he could see a row of red lamps across the road. As he drew nearer he perceived that there was a policeman on each kerb, swinging a lantern. He grinned. He could discern no other obstruction but the lamps in the road. Did they think they could stop him with a few lamps?

He charged the lamps at full speed, and not until he had scattered them did he see what lay behind them. The police had written 'Welcome' on the mat for him. The mat was three feet wide and it stretched across the road from wall to wall. The welcome was in the form of strong steel spikes which protruded from the mat. There were many hundreds of spikes. They could not be avoided.

He shouted a warning, and applied his brakes. He held the wheel in an iron grip, but with torn tyres, at fifty miles an hour, the van was impossible to control. It lurched, veered, and ran full tilt at a women's dress shop on the opposite corner.

The Plumber just managed to avoid a head-on shock. He struck the side of the shop doorway, carrying away the support and shattering two big windows. He was shaken, but not badly hurt. The cab was knocked out of shape and both doors had flown open. He took his gun from his pocket, and he was about to jump down into the road when the sound of shots made him change his mind. The boys were fighting it out with the police. Well, he had told them "Every man for himself." So long as he did not show himself, everyone would assume that he was still in the cab, and seriously injured. The police could not come and look for him while Hannah and Co. were shooting at them. Not for a while, at any rate.

He squeezed out of the cab on the driver's side, which was screened from observation by the bulk of the van. Beside him was the darkened shop window, with all its glass shattered. There were dummy figures of girls in the window wearing the new winter coats. Some of the figures had been knocked over; some were still standing. The getaway specialist stood with them for a moment, considering. There was bound to be a back door, and the police had not yet had time to surround the place. He turned and vanished into the darkness of the shop.

CHAPTER SEVENTEEN

MACFARLANE fired the first shots of the gunfight, but it was Hannah who proved to be the most formidable opponent of the police. He became so engrossed in the business of trying to kill policemen that he never noticed how many of his mates fought beside him. At the end, for a little while, he fought alone.

Bowie, that razor-slashing hooligan, never really fought at all. He had no sense of comradeship and he never even considered staying with his mates. In a panic because he did not know how to escape, he fired a few wild shots and then he turned to ask the Plumber what he should do. He found that the Plumber had gone. He also found that the light-weight upper structure of the van had been torn away from the more solid body of the cab. There was an opening on the same side as the driver's seat, and just behind it. Weak with fright because he was cornered and leaderless, he pushed through the opening and dropped to the ground just at the spot where the Plumber had stood a few seconds before. And like the Plumber he faded into the darkness of the shop.

MacFarlane fought until the time came to insert his last clip of cartridges into his Mauser pistol. As he did so he became aware that Bowie had departed. He looked at Hannah, who was shooting coolly and interestedly, more like a man absorbed in a game of darts than a cornered gunman. He felt contempt for Hannah. Let him be the mug: let him hold the fort for a bit! This thought was followed by wild anger against Bowie. When he found that the Plumber also had fled, his rage increased. He quite forgot that the Plumber had said: "Every man for himself." He cursed the Plumber, and Bowie as well. They had worked a fast one on Alex MacFarlane! They had sold him the dummy; left him to carry the can back!

With no word to Hannah, MacFarlane made his way out through the opening which Bowie had found. He dropped to the ground, and found himself in concealment near the front of the van. He peered around, half expecting to see Bowie or the Plumber lurking there. The clever bastards, leaving him behind! Which way had they gone?

He decided that they had sneaked a little way along the street and dived into the alley which cut through the block. He crouched down besides the front wing of the van, looking along the street. Now the police were closing in on that side also. He could see their shadowy figures moving from doorway to doorway on both sides of the street. But they had not yet seen him, and they had not reached the alley. He thought he could beat them to it. He ran, light-footed and silent.

Nobody fired at him, and he began to think that his movements had not been observed. He went scudding into the alley, straight into the arms of a uniformed policeman. The policeman, who had seen him coming, made no mistake. Big fingers closed on the little man's pistol, and as he involuntarily turned up his face to look at his tall opponent

167

the stiffened edge of a hand flashed up and hit him in the throat. This most painful of blows temporarily robbed him of the ability to breathe, and it was followed by a hard downward-chopping fist which caught him on the left temple and dazed him. He was, after all, only a very small man though a tough one. He relinquished the pistol. The P.C. put the pistol in his pocket. He backed his prisoner against the wall, and handcuffed him. He was well pleased with himself: he was unarmed, and he had disarmed and arrested one of 'the gang', though a little 'un to be sure. He was delighted with MacFarlane for falling into his hands. There was no more rough treatment. He was kindness itself, and when his dispirited prisoner asked for a cigarette he gave him one and lit it for him.

When MacFarlane fled from the van, Hannah soon became aware that he was alone. At the same time, he discovered that he had fired his last round of ammunition. He was suddenly robbed of the sense of power which the gun had given him, and he felt lonely, afraid, and helpless. The realization of his plight so disconcerted him that he rose to his feet, empty gun in hand. It was a fatal mistake. Before he could turn away to the back of the van he fell a victim to Devery, who had crawled on hands and knees along the other, undamaged, frontage of the shop until he reached the corner. The sergeant's bullet, fired upward from a range of three or four yards, penetrated Hannah's brain and killed him instantly.

Hannah died as he had lived, alone. From adolescence he had been a man with no real home, no real friends, no wife, and no children who knew him as their father. He went unmourned, except by Devery. And only by Devery when he examined Hannah's old, sawn-off Webley and ejected six empty cartridges into his hand. He realized that he had killed an unarmed man, and he was filled with remorse. But remorse did not prevent him from replacing three of the empty shells with three unused ones from his own ·45. He did not want the coroner, the Press, or the public to start entertaining the idea that the police had shot a man when he was in the act of surrender.

Martineau was far from being satisfied with the result of the fight at the cross-roads. He still had no knowledge of the whereabouts of three members of a gang which was now known to have been ten in number. Carew and Hannah were dead. MacFarlane and Whitehead were under arrest. Blundell had been reported safe home by the man left on watch there, and officers were on their way to arrest him. Flint and another man had also been seen to arrive home by the observer on the roof of the Tivoli Cinema, and they too would soon be arrested. The man with Flint could be either Beadle, Bowie or Novak, but not Connor. Connor was distinguishable by his size. If, as Martineau suspected, a man had dropped from the van in Darktown at the beginning of the chase, then Connor and one other man had escaped after the van had crashed. And, it seemed, one of those two was carrying a sackful of money.

* * * * *

After groping about in the gloomy interior of the dress shop, the Plumber found an inner door which admitted him to some sort of chamber in which the darkness was absolute. No windows, he decided. Or if there were windows, they were heavily curtained. He used his torch, and found that he was in a short narrow passage—the passage which led to the back door. He strode to the door and examined it, and grunted with relief. Besides being bolted at top and bottom, the door was locked. But the key was in the lock. The way out was clear.

The Plumber's hand was on the key when he stopped, and remained quite still. Behind him he could hear the faint squeak of the inner door which he had just closed. Listening and scarcely breathing, he heard it close again, very quietly.

He turned, with gun extended, and stood with his back to the wall of the passage. "Who's there?" he asked in a whisper.

"It's me, Caps," came the reply. "Don't shoot."

The Plumber switched on his torch and saw Bowie standing with his back to the inner door, with his gun ready in his hand.

The Plumber put the beam of the torch on the back door, for Bowie's benefit. "Come on," he said. "Open this and let's get out of here."

His lip curled as he watched Bowie. The man was clumsy with fear. But he got the door open and led the way outside. There was a wide backyard which served several shops, and the yard gate opened into the cross-alley which bisected the block at right angles to the alley which ran through into Boyton Road. The cross-alley was deserted. A few yards away, at the junction of the two alleys, there was a street light mounted on a wall bracket. The quietness of the place was emphasized by the racket of gunfire out in the main street.

"We'll have to risk being seen passing under that lamp,'" said the Plumber.

He ran to the corner and peeped. The alley was deserted also, because there had still not been time for the police to surround the block. He ran at top speed along the cross-alley, away from the sound of firing, and Bowie ran at his heels. No sooner had they gone than a policeman entered the alley at the far end. He was the man who arrested MacFarlane.

The two fugitives ran along a street of tall office buildings which was at right angles to Boyton Road. The street led them to Union Street, and from there, for a time, they were in the open. Here there were no alleys, and no backyards. They came to Lacy Street and flitted across it like two dark wraiths, and then they felt safe among the narrow but important streets which criss-crossed that part of the city. They came to a square with a big traffic island, and then they were in the open again.

Breathing heavily, they stood for a moment in a shop doorway. They had run more than half a mile. Nothing moved around the square, and all was quiet. Very surprised that they had seen no policemen, they parted company. The Plumber went furtively along one side of the square, and Bowie slunk along the other. Two minutes after they had gone, a police van came rushing into the square. It stopped, and policemen poured out of it. They were the men of the second emergency squad, who recently had been blocking off the Old Cemetery. For weeks afterwards those, men grumbled—when no superior officer was listening—. about the waste of their time and talent on the night of: the Economic job. Tearing around like scalded cats, and then, waiting to catch somebody who wasn't there! While the, C.I.D. and the motor patrols were hogging all the glory!

The Plumber reached home without further trouble. The weary watcher in the little park, still standing with his back to a tree, was surprised to see him walk calmly along the street and go up to his flat. But no lights appeared in the flat. Mr. Connor went to bed in the dark, if he did go to bed. The man in the park thought that he might be sitting at a window, looking out. The man remained as still as possible, but he spoke into his field radio and informed Headquarters that Connor was home.

Neither was Bowie intercepted by the police, but he had other enemies. As he reconnoitred the vicinity of his own street before he walked the last hundred yards to safety, he discerned two motionless figures standing in a house doorway. His nerves jumped with shock when he saw them. He was worn out with the strain of the last two hours, and this disappointment, after a successful escape, sent his spirits down to zero. He leaned wearily against a wall, and wondered dully how this situation had come about. The cops were waiting for him, therefore he had been identified somehow. They knew that he was one of the Plumber's gang, therefore all security was gone. Martin Bowie was on the run.

He turned to go, without first gliding back from the corner where he stood. For a fraction of a second he showed himself, and the movement was seen. The two men emerged from their doorway and ran towards him. He heard the swift patter of their feet as he fled. Then he heard a clear whistle, and it was not a police whistle. He thought he knew that whistle, and when he reached the first corner he was sure he knew. He looked round, and saw his pursuers running under the light of a street lamp. One of them was Dixie Costello. The other was the Dog.

So the boys were after him, and he did not need to be a

thought reader to know that their intentions were hostile. There were more than two of them, because Dixie had certainly not been whistling up the Dog. Four or five of them, including Dixie himself, had stayed out until the small hours waiting for him, so it was evident that their reasons for getting hold of him were urgent. Dixie knew, then! Somehow he had found out that one of his men was a member of the Plumber's gang. Bowie fled on wings of fear, thinking of Dixie's rage.

At this stage, when he was in danger of being overtaken by men who had not run half a mile as he had, his fear of Dixie was greater than his fear of the police. The police would give him a trial, but Dixie and the boys had already tried him. Now they were seeking to implement the sentence. They would carve him with razors and kick and bludgeon him to death. The Dog was there. That cruel devil!

Then he realized that he had one advantage. He had a gun, and the Costello mob did not normally carry guns. At the next corner he stopped, turned, and fired at a running figure. He waited round the corner for a second or two, then he showed himself and fired again. He ran on. That would slow them up a bit, he thought.

He was running into a district which he knew well, because he used to live there. His wife, Ella, still lived there. He found himself running instinctively towards Ella's place, like a boy running home. Then the thought came that he could hide there. Ella would not turn him away at a time like this. Not when he told her that his life was in danger. After all, she was still his wife.

He stopped again, and fired a few shots. Then he doubled around back streets and managed to arrive unseen at Ella's street door. He entered the lobby and closed the door behind him. But he could not secure it, because there was neither key nor bolt. The outer door of that house of flats and furnished rooms was never locked. He went quietly up the stairs to Ella's door. Gently he tried it, and found it locked. He tapped on the door with subdued urgency.

Ella was sleeping lightly, and the gentle, insistent tapping on the door woke her immediately. She felt no resentment at being disturbed, because she thought that the person at the door was Devery. She was out of bed in an instant.

She switched on the light and went into the living-room, and then she stopped. What would Devery think of her if she opened her door in the middle of the night without asking the name of the caller? "Who's there?" she called softly.

"It's me, Martin," came the reply. "Let me in. Let me in for mercy's sake. I'm in mortal danger."

That rat! Her lip curled. Likely enough the police were after him. "Who's chasing you?" she wanted to know.

"The boys. Let me in, quick. For God's sake, Ella."

She reflected. Whatever the trouble was about, Dixie and the boys would not kill Caps. They would lame him, maim him, carve him up, but they would not kill him. She wanted him dead. She had planned his death.

She fumbled with the door. She rattled the key in the lock, but she did not turn it.

"I can't open the door," she said, barely loud enough for him to hear. "The key seems to be stuck. You'll have to put your shoulder to it."

The thought of Dixie and the Dog gave him strength. He drew back, took a little run at the door, and burst the flimsy lock. The door flew open and he lurched into the room. Then he saw Ella. She was just taking something from a drawer in the cupboard beside the fireplace. He saw, to his amazement, that it was a small revolver. She pointed it at him.

"Meet my friend," she said in a voice scarcely louder than a whisper. "He's been waiting for you."

She was smiling. She smiled as she lifted her head slightly, opened her mouth, and screamed. Then he knew that she was not afraid of him, and never had been afraid of him. Her show of terror whenever she saw him had been an act, a build-up. The injunction to restrain him from approaching her had been part of the build-up. She was not afraid of him, but everybody was quite sure that she went in mortal terror of him. She had planned it all, in readiness for an occasion like this. She had even tricked him into bursting open the door.

The smile remained on her scarred face as she continued

to scream. It broadened as her left hand seized the neckline of her thin nightdress and ripped it down, revealing to him the lovely body about which he had dreamed during long nights in Farways prison. He stood like a man petrified, unable to believe that she would actually shoot him. But she did shoot him. She fired six bullets into him, and when he was dead she took his razor from his pocket and put it beside his hand. Her smile faded momentarily as she studied the effect. 'Don't overdo it,' she thought, and she replaced the razor in his pocket. She screamed steadily until the first of the neighbours arrived. If the neighbour observed any trace of her smile, no doubt he thought that she was hysterical. A bit off her head, like, poor lass.

* * * * *

There was quite a list of police injuries, from broken fingers to serious bullet wounds, but no officer had been killed. The Chief Constable was relieved, and determined that now there would be no more men put on the sick list. Six men and two policewomen were sent to pick up Owen Blundell and his sister, and they were joined by the observer who had been lurking in the doorway of a little Noncomformist chapel along the street. No fewer than eight men were sent to get Flint and his guest, and they too were joined by the observer from the cinema roof. He made his way stiffly down the fire escape and announced that he was going to see some action at last, even if he got killed. Without showing themselves, six men surrounded Connor's place, but they awaited the order to go in and take him. On the telephone, Martineau had insisted that he would go for Connor. "I want him alive," he said. "But I'm not ready for him yet."

At Headquarters, Superintendent Clay was worried about evidence. "What have we got?" he bawled into the telephone. "They were seen to leave home, they were followed and lost, and they were seen to come back. They might have been tomcatting for all we can prove. They wore gloves, and all the time they were in action they wore black clouts on their faces. We can't identify any of 'em except the dead 'uns—and maybe MacFarlane."

"We've got a laboratory, haven't we?" retorted Martineau, in no mood to be diplomatic. "They've been in that van, and we'll find evidence on their clothes and their shoes. I daresay we'll be able to prove that they've been in the Eco and the cemetery, too. That wall they climbed, and the gravestones they stumbled over, are covered with lichen and stuff. Then we'll have the guns, and the masks. And we'll have somebody in possession of the boodle when we find him."

"Ah, when!" Clay grumbled. "And what direct evidence is a gun and a black scarf?"

"We have bullets, embedded in police cars which were fired upon. And we have a bullet from the body of Ewart Thompson. Don't forget we have four murders to clear. Wait till I get on about murder with young Blundell. If I can't make him talk his head off I'll put my ticket in. When he knows the game is up, that boy will sing like a nightingale."

"I hope you're right," was the fretful rejoinder. "If this job turns out to be as big a mess as it is right now, I might take you up about that ticket."

"You can have it," said Martineau.

The police who went for Blundell drove up in two cars, and 'covered' the little house in Shirwell back and front. The sergeant in charge pounded on the front door. A light was switched on in one of the bedrooms, and a minute later a window was opened. The head and shoulders of an elderly woman appeared at the window. The sergeant did not have to speak to her. "I'll come down," she said, quietly and calmly.

But there was some delay. A detective pressed open the letter box with his thumb, and put his ear to the aperture. He could hear loud, agitated whispers and the sound of hurried movement. "He's trying to crawl under the carpet," somebody said.

Then the woman came to the door and opened it. She was sturdy and erect in an old blue dressing-gown, and she seemed to bar the way. The sergeant did not ask any questions. He was not going to ask a mother to betray her son. "I'm seeking Owen Blundell and his sister, and I also have a warrant to search this house," he said. "Let me pass, please."

Stony-faced, the woman stood aside. Then she raised an automatic pistol, which she was holding by the barrel, and offered it to the sergeant. He thanked her gravely, and put the pistol in his pocket.

The woman stood watching while the detectives searched the ground floor and the tiny cellar. When the sergeant led the way upstairs she followed. Her hand went to her mouth when she saw him raise the lid of a blanket box, but she uttered no sound.

Blundell was crouching in the blanket box, in an attitude which robbed his surrender of any vestige of dignity. "Come on, get out," said the sergeant. He took the young man by the scruff of the neck and pulled him up.

Grace Blundell had heard her brother come home, and she had thought that all was well. The last job finished, and no more to do. She had snuggled down in bed and mused luxuriously about Positano, Taormina, Paris, Venice; the smart hotels; the hotel bedrooms, with the man she loved. She had fallen happily asleep.

The sergeant's thundering knock on the door had awakened her. The repeated blows sent her dream hotels tumbling in ruins. She knew what this was; the end of everything between herself and Robert Connor. It might even be the end of Robert himself. She slipped out of bed and looked through the window. Her room was at the back of the house. She saw men at the back gate. Policemen, of course.

She crept back to bed, and curled up small. She shivered, though the bed was warm. She was one of those who believed that the police had an almost supernatural way of finding out things. So after the first shock she had no feeling of surprise. She told herself, now, that all the time she had foreseen the end of this. She should never have listened to Robert, never have allowed him to make her think that he was cleverer than the police. She should have stopped him, days or weeks ago. She should have made him take her away, and all would have been well. Now, if he escaped, she would never see him again. If he did not escape, he would go to prison for years and years.

She did not think of what might happen to herself until the door was opened and the light switched on. She raised herself on one elbow, expecting to see her mother. She saw two policewomen in uniform. "Come along," one of the policewomen said kindly. "Get up and get dressed. You're wanted at Headquarters."

White and expressionless, the widow Blundell saw first her son and then her daughter taken away by the police. Neither of them spoke to her, or looked at her, as they were led away. Such a parting must have been pure heart-break for her. Perhaps she wondered then if she was the one at fault, for giving them too much of their own way and too much from her meagre resources when they were children: too much love, though they had never shown love for her except when they wanted something. Perhaps she did not think of that at all, being too numbed by the calamity which she had foreseen and awaited, though certainly it could not have been so great a shock as when the police came for Owen the first time, when she had suspected nothing. Perhaps, indeed, she had no feeling but relief, for the end of the worry and the waiting.

Two detectives were left behind to search the house. They were most considerate in their treatment of Mrs. Blundell. She did not speak to them, but when the first grey of dawn appeared in the sky she made tea, and took it to them.

* * * * *

Flint and Novak gave the police even less trouble than Blundell. The two men were drinking coffee and talking over the events of the night when the knock came. Flint said: "Hell, they musta followed us." There was a brief delay while guns wrapped in black kerchiefs were hastily hidden, and then Flint answered the door. Four detectives crowded into his crummy, smelly living-room, driving him before them. His remarks about 'a free country' and 'a fine time of night' were ignored. The guns were quickly found. Flint was still protesting when he was taken away. Novak said nothing, but he looked very unhappy.

The detectives who were left to search the place also looked rather unhappy. There were sounds upstairs as of an elephant stirring. Mrs. Flint was awake. They knew that while they searched they would have to listen to a running commentary from a foul-mouthed harridan who would enjoy the expression of her hatred for them.

CHAPTER EIGHTEEN

By three o'clock Martineau was—as he phrased it—beginning to get organized. He had all the available information, and he still needed to locate one man and a sackful of currency. He summed up. Carew and Whitehead, the Plumber's drivers, had never even seen the money. It had not been found in the van after Hannah's death, and MacFarlane had not been carrying it when he was arrested. Flint, Novak, Blundell and Connor had all been seen by observers as they arrived home, and none of them had been carrying a bulky sack. Bowie had been chased by men thought to be members of the Costello mob. The police observer had witnessed the very beginning of the chase, and Bowie had not been in possession of a sack. He had been killed by his wife, and there was no sack or bundles of notes in her flat. Therefore the one man unaccounted for was holding the money. And that man was almost certainly Beadle.

Martineau did not accept this theory as absolute truth. The money could have been hidden by another man during flight. And because of this, a great deal of leg work was going on. The probable lines of flight of Blundell, Flint, Novak, Connor and Bowie had been plotted, and men were searching along those lines.

With that work in progress, and Connor pent up in his flat, the chief inspector felt free to seek the money in his own way. He thought that the place to look for Beadle was Darktown. When he recollected the movements of the stolen van in Darktown, and its subsequent movements, he was aware of a sort of pattern. It would be typical conduct of the Plumber to get rid of his loot as soon as possible, and then to lead his pursuers away from the place where he had left it. After that, he had tried to ensure that himself and the rest of the gang escaped. His design for that escape had been surprisingly successful. Only one man had been captured when the van was stopped, and one man killed. If the police had not already known the names of the gang's members, most of them would have got clean away.

Martineau decided to try and follow the Plumber's route through Darktown again. For that purpose he wanted the same car crew as before; the original driver, Devery, Detective Constable Derbyshire, and himself.

He sent for the other three. They came, eager-eyed and untired, still anxious to distinguish themselves and gain promotion. "Are we going after the cash, sir?" Devery wanted to know.

Martineau nodded. "We've got to find it, too. If we don't, I'll be in trouble for acting a bit too previous. We could have left some of those thieves free and under observation, hoping that they'd lead us to the cash. That is what our venerable seniors will say."

"I'll confess that the idea occurred to me, sir."

"After a scare like this, with the newspapers screaming their heads off about a quarter of a million stolen money, they wouldn't go near the money for a month. I can't wait that long. I'm going to clear this job tonight. It's been a bit untidy so far, but it'll straighten out."

"I'm sure it will," said Devery loyally. "Where do we start?"

"The Belmont Transport Café, where they picked up the van," said Martineau.

They set out on their journey. At the café a witness was found. He had seen a number of men around the van just before it was stolen. "It was dark, like," he explained. "I thought the old Bedford 'ud had a bump and they were looking at it." He admitted that he had not seen one of the men holding a sack.

When he heard that, Martineau spoke to Headquarters and arranged to have the whole of the Old Cemetery searched, and also the alleys and backyards along the streets between the cemetery and the café.

Then the four men went to Darktown. At first they had no difficulty in tracing the original route, but when they were among the little streets which looked so much alike there were disagreements. Sometimes they had to stop the car while they decided whether the van had gone this way or that, but little of the route was missed.

Men made their comments as they went along. "Spider Normington lives next door to that little shop," Derbyshire remarked on one occasion. "He's good enough for anything."

"Bear that in mind," said Martineau. "We might have to be seeing Spider."

Devery groaned. "There's dozens of Spiders living around here. Any one of 'em would harbour a man like Beadle if it was a paying proposition."

"I keep looking for cover, but I don't see any," said Derbyshire. "Every door opens straight on to the street. There's not a bit of a garden wall or a dark backyard or anything."

"Every house is cover, that's the devil of it," was the sergeant's rejoinder. "If a door was left unlocked, Beadle could drop off the van and nip into a house in about two seconds flat."

After that there was silence in the car, until Derbyshire remarked: "That's the first bit of cover I've seen."

"Where?" Martineau demanded sharply.

"That little boozer we just passed. There's a yard at the side."

"Stop the car when you've turned the corner," said Martineau to the driver. "I seem to remember something about a little pub in Darktown. About five years ago. The licensee was up on a receiving charge, but he got away with it. We'll just walk back and see what's stirring."

They left the car and walked quietly back to the inn.

When they reached the opening which led to the yard at the rear, Martineau stopped them. He went and looked around the yard, and returned.

"This is a right cosy place," he said. "We'll see if there's anybody here who can't sleep."

He sent Derbyshire to the back door, with instructions to stand well back so that he could see both door and windows. Then he went and stood across the street with Devery and the driver. The three men faced the tavern in a line, so that they could see every window.

"Now keep your eyes open," the inspector said. "Curiosity killed the cat. I'm going to make some noise."

He coughed quite loudly, then he said conversationally: "Arriwar abat seven." He waited a moment, and then he said: "Gerrand ther. Yulla sinim."

There was absolute silence in the street. Nobody and nothing moved. Then Martineau coughed again.

Straining his eyes to see, Devery thought that he perceived a pale blur well back behind an uncurtained window of the tavern. He saw it appear and disappear. It could have been a white face dimly seen; a face which did not often see the sun, or one upon which the prison pallor still remained.

"Did you see anything?" he whispered.

"Something moved at that bedroom window on the left," said the driver.

"That's it," said Martineau with satisfaction. "I saw it too. We'll turn this place up. We don't need a warrant to search licensed premises."

He told the driver to stay where he was, in a position to see the entire front of the tavern and the passage to the backyard. He went across the street with Devery and pounded on the front door.

There was no answer. The place was as silent as a tomb.

Martineau's fist thundered on the door again. "Wake up!" he shouted. And when there was no answer he kicked the door.

At last a light was switched on in the room where the face had been seen. A window was opened. "What do you want?"

181

a woman asked. But she was not angry, or even irritable. The quaver of fear was in her voice.

"This is the police," said Martineau. "Go back to bed, madam, and send your husband down to open this door."

"I—I can't send him down. He's poorly in bed."

"Better come down yourself, then. I have reason to believe that you are harbouring a wanted criminal."

"Nay, Mister!" said the woman reproachfully. Then she added: "I'm not sure whether you're bobbies or not."

"You'll know in a minute, if you don't open this door," Martineau promised her.

She came down and opened the door. She was younger than Martineau had expected, and even aroused from bed she had a certain blowsy attractiveness. But she was in a sad state of nerves.

The two policemen entered the tavern. Martineau locked the front door and put the key in his pocket, while Devery went to the back door and pocketed the key. "Now," said the inspector. "What's the matter with your husband?"

"Er, he's got bronchitis. He has to stop in bed."

"Right. I'll have a look at him. Lead the way, please."

Leaving Devery at the foot of the stairs, Martineau followed the woman up to the bedroom. A man lay in the double bed, with sheets up to his neck. His eyes were closed. His face was pale, and he did look rather ill.

"Wake up," said Martineau, not unkindly. "You've got visitors."

The man opened his eyes. "What's the matter? Who're you?" he asked in a weak voice.

Martineau gave his name. He had never set eyes on the man before, but he remarked: "I seem to know your face. Weren't you once acquitted on a charge of receiving?"

"Receiving what? I don't know what you're talking about."

"I think you do. What ails you?"

There was a perceptible hesitation, then the man said: "I'm crippled with rheumatics."

"Well, see if you can get out of bed."

"I can't."

"You were out of bed five minutes ago."

"I wasn't," the man said. "That was my wife." He gave the woman a baleful look.

Martineau stepped forward and threw the covers back. "Get up," he said. "And get your pants on."

The man groaned as he got off the bed. He put on trousers and slippers.

"Right," said Martineau. "Now show me round. Imagine I'm buying the place."

The man obeyed. He did his best to ignore the door of one bedroom, but his unwelcome visitor said: "We'll try this as well. You go first."

In the room they found Beadle, fully dressed. He was too old a hand to try anything silly like hiding under the bed or in the wardrobe. He was sitting on a stool beside the fireplace, awaiting his fate. He dejectedly admitted his identity, and when Martineau asked about stolen money he went and pulled a sack from beneath the bed. "It's all there," he said.

"We'll know that when it's counted," said Martineau. "Where's your gun?"

"No gun, boss. I never carried a gun in me life."

Martineau tapped the peterman's pockets, and nodded. Then he picked up the sack and felt the weight of it. "A nice haul," he said.

"What is it?" the landlord asked.

Martineau looked at him. "I think it'll be stolen money. Hundreds of thousands of pounds."

"How did that get here? When I gave this man shelter for the night, he didn't have a sack with him. Somebody must have passed it up to him. I don't have dealings with robbers."

"Hello, hello," said Beadle. "Somebody's ratting already."

The landlord glared. "I tell you I'm no robber!"

Beadle returned the glare. "You ain't no flaming pink-winged angel, neither!" he snarled.

Martineau was listening intently to the bickering, and Beadle suddenly realized it. He closed his mouth and set his lips.

Martineau noticed the change of expression.

"So you won't talk," he derided. "The last of the dauntless three. The last of the round dozen, come to think of it. Your pal Carew is on the slab, as dead as mutton. So are John Hannah and Caps Bowie. The others are in the cooler, wondering what they're going to say to the judge. I'll tell you their names, so you'll know I'm not kidding. MacFarlane, Whitehead, Blundell, Flint, Novak and Connor. Oh, and Egan. And now we've got you, the man with the money. It's just possible that you might have to carry the can back for the whole mob. They'll make you do it, if they can."

Beadle sat down heavily on the bed. It seemed that Martineau's glib recital of names had shaken him.

"Who was the canary?" he asked. "Whitehead?"

Martineau smiled. "Why ask? You know we don't divulge sources of information. That's why it might be possible for you, and our friend the landlord, to make yourself clean, as clean as a whistle."

Beadle pointed to the sack of currency. "With that around? Who're you kidding?"

"Oh, you won't get away from that, of course. I'm referring to something else. Murder."

The others did not speak, and Martineau went on: "I was there when Ewart Thompson was murdered. He died in my arms, as they say. You were there too. You were on that job, Beadle, and you know who killed Thompson. You're involved. Just think that over. Don't say anything right now. Just think it over."

Beadle did not think it over. With a lifetime's hatred of the police in his voice he said: "I *will* say something right now. I wouldn't tell you the time if I had fifty gold watches."

Martineau was not really disappointed. It was what he had expected of Beadle. It would be a different story, he thought, when he began to question this white-faced innkeeper, and young Blundell, and his sister, and Luke Whitehead. They did not have the iron fatalism of a man like Beadle.

* * * * *

Martineau went to get Robert Connor. The Plumber, undoubtedly the Plumber. The murdering schemer who had rifled the city, and caused him weeks and weeks of work and worry.

With the Economic job 'wrapped up', the chief inspector could call upon plenty of men. He made sure of Connor. He put two dozen armed plainclothes men around Park Terrace, and they were picked men. They were picked because they all knew Connor by sight, having known him when he was a successful man of law. There was to be no chance, in the darkness, of someone mistaking Connor for a fellow officer.

Martineau went up to the flat himself, and Devery and Derbyshire went with him. He was prepared for trouble, but he was not expecting it. Connor was a lawyer. When cornered, he would seek the legal way out. His next fight would be in court, under the eyes of a stipendiary magistrate.

Normally—if ever such circumstances could be called normal—Connor would have behaved as Martineau supposed he would. He would have bluffed, playing the part of an outraged gentleman and threatening legal retaliation. There was no stolen property in the flat, and no suspiciously large amount of money. There was a black silk kerchief, but even if forensic scientists could prove that it had been worn across the nose and mouth, it was not damning evidence. But there *was* damning evidence; a Biretta automatic pistol, one of a pair. Connor had not used it since he had shot Ewart Thompson with it, and he had intended to throw it away. He had neglected to do so. The absolutely safe disposal of a murder weapon is nearly always a problem. Connor had not yet made the decision about that, and the pistol was still in the flat.

Martineau did not knock on the door: he charged it with his shoulder. The door withstood the first onslaught, and Connor, who had been lying on his settee, sprang up and dived across the room. He switched on the light and shot the bolts which had been fitted at top and bottom of the door. Then he went to put on his shoes, which were lying on the floor beside the settee. He knew immediately that he would have to run, if he could. That pistol was something which could not be explained away.

Martineau took another run at the door, and cracked a panel. He shattered the cracked panel with his foot. He could see into the room: he and Connor faced each other for the first time. Connor, having tied his shoe-laces, switched off the light.

Martineau smashed a second panel of the door. He reached through and began to grope for the lower bolt. Connor pushed a heavy chest of drawers against the door, nearly trapping the policeman's arm.

The hunted man opened one of the drawers and took out his two Birettas, the murder weapon and the one which he had used that night. He put one in each side pocket of his coat. Then he ran to the window and drew the curtains aside. He raised the lower pane as far as it would go, and climbed out on to the sill. A foot away from the window there was a fall pipe. He hoped that it would be firm enough to bear his weight, but he had no time to worry about it. He began to climb up the pipe, an exercise in which he had had no practice. He got to the top because he could not afford to fail. He was exhausted when he finally scrambled on to the roof.

He lay on the slates for a minute or two, getting his breath. He could hear men calling excitely to each other. He reflected that the police, having of course observed him, would be seeking the top floor, and a skylight. He crawled up the roof to the apex, where there was a chimney stack. First, he thought, get rid of this damned incriminating pistol. He stood up beside the stack, with his left arm around the chimney pot. The pistol was not loaded, and it had been in his mind to drop it down a chimney, trusting to luck that it would lodge in a bend. But now he had a better idea.

He looked down upon the park, and at the houses beyond. Straight across the road, in the park, was a dense shrubbery. From that elevation he could not miss it. The pistol might lie among shrubs until the leaves of autumn covered it completely. It might never be found. At any rate it would not be found until the man who threw it there was far away.

The skyline beyond the park was showing the first grey light of dawn. Therefore, Connor knew, his silhouette would be visible to men standing in the back street behind him. If he raised his arm they would see the action, and later one of them would interpret it correctly. He did not raise his arm. He set his feet firmly on the slope and the apex, clasped the chimney pot, and threw the pistol with an underarm action. He stood listening for a moment. There was no sound of the pistol landing in the road, so it must have reached the shrubbery.

With the pistol disposed of, Connor turned his mind to the problem of escaping the police. He had a chance, he thought. It was a fine night. One or two skylights would be open. He would drop down into somebody's attic and make his way down to the street door. He would beat down any opposition. If he had to use his pistol, he would do so.

He scrambled along the steep roof, clinging to the ridge tile. How on earth had the police located him so quickly, he wondered. That some of his men could be made to talk after arrest, he did not doubt. But not immediately. MacFarlane and Hannah might be under arrest, but neither of them would 'grass'. Carew and Whitehead might be under arrest, also, but all the others had got safely away. Whitehead. It must be Whitehead. Connor decided that he would kill Whitehead if ever he had the opportunity.

It was hardly likely that he would even see Whitehead again. If he got out of this trap he would have to make straight for the coast, for the little yachting resort where his boat was lying. Thank God for the boat. He could get across to Ireland with it, to a little fishing village which he had often visited. He was known and respected there; known and respected as Mr. William Porteous.

He found an open skylight, and tried to calculate whose it might be. He could not remember, because he had never taken the trouble to learn and memorize in which particular flats his neighbours lived. The skylight moved easily on its hinges, and he propped it wide open. Then, crouching, he held his torch down inside the room and switched it on. There was a single bed, and a flaxen head on the pillow. A little girl, or a small boy. He hoped it was a boy A girl would scream the house down.

He dropped into the attic, and flashed his light around to find the door. As he went out he turned to look at the occupant of the bed. It was a boy, with his head raised, blinking sleepily at the light of the torch.

He went down a few steps, into what appeared to be the living-room of a top-floor flat. He found the door and let himself out. As he went down the stairs he heard a woman calling: "Charlie!" She probably thought that little Charlie had fallen out of bed and landed on his head.

At the street door Connor paused in shadow. It was no good. While he hesitated a man ran up and flashed a light on him. He charged down the three steps of the entrance and kicked out murderously. The man avoided his foot, and caught it in his hand and helped it on its upward way. Connor fell on the steps, but he also drew in his foot. When the man dived at him the foot shot out and caught him in the lower part of the chest. He fell on his back. He tried to rise but he was evidently injured.

Connor was up, but new opposition had appeared. This was a very big man. That fellow Martineau! Connor went for his gun.

Martineau was growling in his throat like a wolfhound. He hit Connor, one, two. Connor staggered back and fell on the steps again. He was holding his pistol, but he did not shoot Martineau. The pistol was kicked out of his grasp. He let it go: it was of no use to him, because it was not loaded. Nothing had happened when he had tried to fire it. He did not get up to fight on. He knew that his day was done. He, the man with the brains, the organizer, had in the stress of action made the most elementary mistake of all. He had thrown away the wrong gun.